What happened to her safe and tidy destiny?

"You never told me, Miss MacNeil," Mitch murmured, bringing his face closer to hers, "just what kind of fool put a diamond like that on your finger and then let you run off—to Nashville of all places?"

Dinah looked into his eyes and found them more mesmerizing, more mocking than ever. "Why do you say—Nashville, of all places?"

"Because," he muttered, "one of the things Nashville is about is passion.... Passion," he repeated softly as his lips took hers with a completeness that dazzled her. He drew back. "You kiss like a girl who's been taught never to show her feelings."

She gasped at his arrogance. "I should have slapped your face!"

"But you didn't— Maybe there's hope for you, yet."

Who was this man? What sort of sorcery had he worked on her? She'd been with dependable Dennis all these years and never once had he made her feel this way.

Bethany Campbell, an English major, teacher and textbook consultant, calls her writing world her "hidey-hole," that marvelous place where true love always wins out. Her hobbies include writing poetry and thinking about that little scar on Harrison Ford's chin. She laughingly admits that her husband, who produces videos and writes comedy, approves of the first one only.

Books by Bethany Campbell

Don't miss any of our special offers. Write to us at the following address for information on our newest releases.

Harlequin Reader Service
901 Fuhrmann Blvd., P.O. Box 1397, Buffalo, NY 14240
Canadian address: P.O. Box 603,
Fort Erie, Ont. L2A 5X3

The Diamond Trap

Bethany Campbell

Harlequin Books

TORONTO • NEW YORK • LONDON
AMSTERDAM • PARIS • SYDNEY • HAMBURG
STOCKHOLM • ATHENS • TOKYO • MILAN

ISBN 0-373-02949-7

Harlequin Romance first edition December 1988

CHAPTER ONE

I SHOULDN'T HAVE COME HERE TODAY, she thought.

But it was too late now. So Dinah stood, the May sunshine burnishing her golden hair. She looked down the mountainside at the small town where she had spent the past nine months of her life, the town she was about to leave forever.

The spring breeze whispered in the nearby sycamore trees. Goodbye, the leaves seemed to say: goodbye, goodbye. Uncomfortable, she shrugged her small shoulders and thrust her hands deep into the pockets of her billowing skirt. Although the aging man who stood beside her was kind, she didn't want to look into his eyes. She continued to stare down into the valley.

From the steps of the small church, Dinah could view most of the dingy buildings of Kakexia. Dominating everything was the dark opening of Draco Mine Number Six. It loomed, yawning, in the side of the coal-dust-blackened mountain, a great dark maw that seemed to threaten to devour anything of beauty the town might produce.

It was Sunday afternoon. The school year was newly over and Kakexia's small population had gathered for a picnic in the ragged little school yard. She should have been there, for the picnic was in part a celebration for her—and for Willard.

She was going home to Connecticut after a year of teaching. Willard was retiring, after giving most of his adult life

to the Kakexia school system. But Willard had asked her to
hike up the slope to the church with him. Dinah was afraid
she knew exactly what he was going to ask her to do.

I shouldn't have come up here, she thought again apprehensively. *I should have said no.*

Below them, men, women and children gathered around
the front of the school, clapping hands and tapping feet.
The school stairs served as a makeshift stage, and three
teenage boys stood on them, making music. Music, Dinah
thought with wonder. In spite of everything the people of
Kakexia never stopped making music.

She swallowed to ease the tightness in her throat and
studied the little band, especially the thin boy in the center.
He was the lead singer and guitarist, sixteen-year-old Roscoe Hockenberry. He wore his best jeans—faded and
patched nonetheless—secondhand cowboy boots, and a
battered white cowboy hat at least two sizes too big for him.
It settled down over his ears, making them stick out like
handles to hold it up.

She sighed. Roscoe. Her favorite student and her most
maddening. In spite of her efforts, he had failed every
course except music. He didn't read well, his math skills
were nonexistent, and he was as unwordly as was possible
for a boy his age. There was no choice for him but to go into
the mines that had killed his father and his elder brother. No
recourse except one. And Dinah knew it was impossible,
anyway.

She swallowed hard again. Although she had grown
deeply fond of all her students, Roscoe had stolen a special
section of her heart. She felt she was abandoning him.

She sensed the watchful eyes of Willard Wakefield on her.
He stood beside her on the church steps. Willard was the
principal and math teacher of the small consolidated school
where Dinah had taught this past year. In his quiet way, he

was the most idealistic man she'd ever met. He was stooped and lean, with a full head of unruly iron-gray hair.

"Happy to be leaving?" Willard questioned. "Or sad?"

"Both," she answered, turning her gaze to his leathery face. "You must be feeling the same thing—only more intense, I imagine."

She had given one short year to Kakexia. Willard had given his life and this was his home in the deepest sense of the word. When she had come, as a government volunteer, she had felt selfless and noble. Now she simply saw how much remained to be done, and she felt like a charlatan for leaving only because her year was up.

"Don't be sad." Willard smiled fondly. "You did a wonderful job. When you arrived, a little bitty thing with your fancy education and fancy clothes, I never thought you'd make it, but you did—with flying colors."

Dinah smiled back gratefully, but could make no reply. She didn't think she had done a wonderful job. After all these months, she was just beginning to understand Kakexia and its problems. There had been too many students she didn't know how to reach. And Roscoe, down there, singing his heart out, had been her most spectacular failure.

Roscoe would descend into the blackness of the mines, and she would return to Connecticut and the good life. Everybody at the country club and the yacht club would tell her how brave and charitable she'd been, and how much good she'd done. Only she would know she hadn't done much good at all.

Dinah turned to Willard, her dark blue eyes locking with his serious, bespectacled ones. She was a petite woman, barely five feet. Her fair hair was cut short, worn straight and practically, a shining helmet of gold. Her face, with its full lips, aristocratic nose and startling sapphire eyes combined delicacy with a beauty that had a strange and unexpected fire. Her loveliness had bloomed this past year, as if Kakexia had matured and perfected her.

The wind shifted slightly and brought the music from the school yard with it. For a few seconds, Roscoe Hockenberry's beautiful, untrained voice wavered like a phantom on the breeze.

"I suppose you're anxious to get back to Connecticut. Get married. Start graduate school, eh?" Willard probed, testing her mood. He looked significantly at the huge engagement ring that sparkled on her left hand. How inappropriate and selfish that ring seemed in Kakexia.

Tell him yes, she lectured herself sternly. Tell him you'll be delighted to go back, to marry Dennis, to start your master's degree at Yale. Tell him, yes, yes, yes, you'll be glad to go home and live the way you were programmed to live.

"No," she said. She had to be honest with Willard. More important, she had to start being honest with herself. "I guess I'm not that eager. I'll miss everybody too much. I'll miss teaching."

Dinah's family enjoyed wealth, prestige and significant political power. Her great-grandfather had established the MacNeil tradition of philanthropy and had set up half a dozen charitable and cultural foundations. His will stipulated that each of his young heirs attend an Ivy League college, donate a year to public service, then take up a position in public service or one of his businesses or foundations. His legacy was one of rewards for virtue and obedience. He was a canny old Scot who planned to keep his empire functioning smoothly and his heirs out of trouble.

So far in her life, Dinah had behaved perfectly and acted according to his decrees. Her school year in Kakexia was her little adventure into harsh reality and her brief education in the difficulties of making the world a better place. She had served her time and paid her dues, at least according to the strictures of her great-grandfather's will.

Now she would go home and marry Dennis, whose family was even richer than hers. Theirs would be the perfect marriage because for years everyone had told her she and Dennis were an ideal pair. She would get a master's in history and automatically be installed as an assistant head of the MacNeil Museum in Hew Haven. This all had been decided years ago, before she'd ever seen Kakexia. Dennis would devote himself to his music and managing his family wealth. Yes, it was a very safe and tidy destiny. Why did it suddenly seem empty?

"Well?" Willard probed, his voice still careful, "You must be anxious to get back to your young man. Dennis, is it?"

Dinah again wished she could say yes. Why shouldn't she be eager to return to Dennis? He was artistic, well educated and considerate to a fault. She and Dennis had been together from childhood. But lately, whenever Dinah thought of marriage, a voice deep within her cried out in warning—*No! Not yet!*

She admitted, "I'm not sure, Willard. I don't think I'm the same person as when I came here. Somehow Kakexia changed me. The students changed me. I need time to think—about everything."

"Umm" was all Willard replied, his tone moody. He stared down at the valley again. "You're lucky because you *can* leave," he said solemnly. "I've tried to get a better life for as many kids as I could." Willard shook his head in frustration. "And I did help a few. Not nearly enough. But a few."

"More than a few, Willard," Dinah said.

"Not nearly enough," he repeated stubbornly. "I've seen too many that didn't have any choice but to stay here and go

into those mines. And they're bad mines, Dinah—the most
dangerous in the state. I hate the damned things."

Dinah hated them, too. Too many men had died in them,
including Roscoe's father and brother, as well as his uncle
and great-uncle. Just as insidious were the respiratory dan-
gers haunting the miners, especially black lung disease.

Dinah understood well the difficulties of coping with
disease. She had been a frail child and had struggled with
recurrent pneumonia every long, cold Connecticut winter.
She was fine now, but her experience made her fear even
more deeply for Roscoe. She watched him in the school
yard, singing with all his might with his strong, young, still-
healthy lungs.

"Dinah, I've got to ask you a favor," Willard rasped.
Embarrassment played across his rough face. "If you're
really not that eager to get back to Connecticut, or your
young man—"

"Yes?" she said apprehensively. *Here it comes,* she
thought.

He cleared his throat awkwardly. "I want you to take
Roscoe to Nashville," he said. "For three weeks. Maybe
longer. So he can find out about the contract."

Dinah's shoulders stiffened. But she said neither yes nor
no. Instead her answer quietly challenged him. "You really
don't believe all that rigmarole about a recording contract,
do you?"

Willard shrugged in bewilderment. "I know these things
aren't supposed to happen in real life—no reputable record
executive walks into a town like this one and offers to sign
up an uneducated, unknown boy like Roscoe."

"And yet you're asking me to let him believe such an offer? Actually take him to Nashville?" Dinah asked, her
heart beating hard.

"It might work out," Willard muttered stubbornly. "I've been on the phone. There really is a Diamond Horseshoe Record Company in Nashville. It really is owned by this Mitch Carey. And he really does want Roscoe to come to Nashville to cut demonstration tapes. It's a chance, Dinah. It can't just be thrown away."

Dinah ran both hands through her smooth blond hair, rumpling it in frustration. Roscoe's so-called recording contract had been the talk of Kakexia ever since a man named Lucky Bucky Williston had turned up over spring break. Dinah had been in Connecticut that week, but she'd heard about the man's visit over and over. Many of the townspeople had been tremendously impressed by Lucky Bucky Williston and the offer he'd made on behalf of Mitch Carey.

But reports of Lucky Bucky had not impressed Dinah. He was a large man, well-fed—portly, people said—who wore an electric-blue cowboy suit and boots made of ostrich skin. He effected a black ten-gallon hat with a gaudy band made of the skins of coral snakes. He drove an electric-blue Cadillac convertible whose horn could play six different tunes, including "Dixie" and "Heartbreak Hotel."

Lucky Bucky Williston said he was in Kakexia because he was on a great talent search for Diamond Horseshoe, and he'd heard people talking about Roscoe Hockenberry and how well he sang; he'd heard it through six counties, in fact.

He had sat in the general store, his thick legs crossed, and listened to a very nervous Roscoe sing only four songs. The big man had recorded them on a tape machine the size of a small refrigerator. Then he smiled fatly and announced to everyone assembled in the store that he and Mitch Carey were going to make Roscoe Hockenberry into a major recording star, a legend in his own time and a very rich man.

Dinah knew vaguely that Nashville was the music capital of the South and its life's blood was the down-home country music Roscoe warbled as naturally as a bird sings. But she also knew that show business anywhere, including Nashville, harbored crooks, cheats and con artists. She doubted that either Lucky Bucky Williston or Mitch Carey was honest. People didn't just drive Cadillacs into obscure little mining towns and offer untold riches to a boy like Roscoe Hockenberry.

There were other people who had been doubtful about the honesty of Lucky Bucky and his equally mysterious employer, Mitch Carey, at least at first. None of the cooler heads in town had trusted the wild promises—and that included Roscoe's widowed mother, Vesta. "No," Vesta had said emphatically. There was no way Roscoe was going to be lured to the wicked city by conniving strangers who were obviously up to no good.

Roscoe became so confused by all the conflicting advice that he did more poorly than usual for the rest of the school year. Dinah privately cursed the unseen Mitch Carey for Roscoe's abysmal failure this past semester.

For Mitch Carey, whoever he was, wasn't willing to take no for an answer. He had bombarded Vesta Hockenberry with telegrams, which terrified her—nobody in Kakexia had ever received telegrams except during wartime, when something tragic had happened.

He kept sending offers—each more enticing than the last. Kakexia was small, so Dinah knew all the details: a thousand dollars plus expenses for Roscoe to come to Nashville for three weeks and make demonstration tapes, with the option for Diamond Horseshoe to produce an album, the contract fee to be negotiated later.

If Vesta Hockenberry was nervous about Roscoe's being alone in Nashville, Mitch Carey himself would put the boy up at his mansion; Mitch Carey himself would recommend the most scrupulous of agents to protect Roscoe's interests; and Mitch Carey himself, in all his generosity, would play host to Vesta or the chaperon of her choice. Dinah had grown angrier and more suspicious at each offer.

At first Vesta remained firm. Roscoe was not going off to Nashville alone, and heaven knew she couldn't take him. Vesta was frightened out of her wits by the thought of a big city and business dealings. Besides, she had his younger sisters to care for. Roscoe's elder sister was married with small children of her own. She couldn't take him.

But Mitch Carey was persistent, if not honest. Vesta grew more bewildered and confused. Dinah began to resent the man and his manipulations with a fervor that surprised her. Without ever showing his face, he had set the town at sixes and sevens, reducing poor Vesta to tears and palpitations and Roscoe to hopeless confusion.

Mitch Carey sensed Vesta's wavering; his onslaughts became more relentless. He began calling and writing to the most prominent people in Kakexia, including Willard.

Throughout it all, Dinah found the offers sinister, too good to be true. Yet others were weakening. Now it had come to this. Willard was actually asking her to take Roscoe to Nashville. She didn't know anything about country music. She'd never even listened to it before she came to Kakexia. She didn't trust Lucky Bucky Williston, and she had come to despise Mitch Carey without even seeing him.

"Why me?" she asked, trying to postpone answering Willard as long as possible. "I've never been to Nashville. I don't know anything about the recording business. I haven't got one single qualification—and I've told you and Roscoe and everybody else, I simply don't believe these people."

Willard shrugged uncomfortably. "It's the consensus," he said gruffly. "You're the best qualified person. You're smart. You learn fast. You're not intimidated by a city—or by people who wield power. Your family has enough clout that Mitch Carey should be very careful of trying to mislead you. But I think—just maybe, Dinah—the man might be honest. He's called me more than once. He sounds sincere. He's promised to help look after Roscoe and any chaperon Vesta deems fit to send with him. She's finally agreed—if *you'll* go to watch out for Roscoe."

I'm supposed to go to Connecticut and plan a very large wedding, Dinah thought dazedly, *not go to Nashville to baby-sit the amiable, immature and innocent Roscoe Hockenberry.*

Willard, having begun his onslaught, charged on. "Vesta trusts you," he said doggedly. "You're one of the few teachers Roscoe's ever actually wanted to please. He likes you, he admires you and he'll listen to you and respect your opinion. I'm too old and inexperienced to go, and besides, my ulcer would turn cartwheels."

Dinah, who knew all about the acrobatics of Willard's famous ulcer, felt guilty and stared down at the schoolhouse. The band was taking a break, tuning their instruments. She could see Roscoe bent studiously over his guitar—far more studiously than he had ever bent over any book.

"Roscoe," Willard said, following her gaze. "He's got talent, Dinah. More than any student I've ever had. I know you don't really understand his music, and I mean no insult when I say I suspect you don't even realize how talented he is." Willard suddenly looked older than his years and infinitely tired. "I want you to get him out of here. You're the only one who can do it. Give him his chance. It may be the only one he ever gets. Take him to Nashville. If not for himself, then for me—he's the boy I wanted to help most of all—and I failed. Completely. Maybe you'll succeed. Otherwise, it's the mines for him.''

Dinah suddenly felt weak, overcome by a sense of fatalism. She didn't think anything awaited Roscoe in Nashville except deception and disappointment. But she would take him—because what Willard said was true. It was the only chance Roscoe had. She didn't want the boy in the mines, either. She owed it to him to help him find any possible avenue of escape.

"We didn't save him with the school system," Willard persisted. "We've got one more try. A long shot. But he does have talent. Lots of it. Are you going to take him, Dinah? Are you going to give him his chance—slim as it might be?"

Dinah looked down into the valley again. This time Roscoe's thin, gangly figure was the only one she saw.

"Yes," she said at last. "I'll take him." Her voice was calm, but she felt as if the earth had tilted slightly, throwing everything awry. Her mother would never understand, and worse, Dennis would pretend to, out of deference to her feelings.

Willard slipped his bony arm around her shoulders and gave her a fatherly hug. "That's my girl," he said. Dinah tried to smile up at him, but couldn't.

What have I got myself into? she wondered helplessly. Roscoe was a sweet boy, charming and unaffected, but he knew practically nothing except his music and the small world of Kakexia. And she had agreed to guide him through the perils of a business she didn't begin to understand. Like the rest of the town, she had fallen under a peculiar enchantment—she wanted to believe in Mitch Carey. Her head knew it was foolish, but her heart yearned to have faith. She realized that she must not be misled, must be utterly cool and reasonable.

Yet, at the same time, she felt slightly drunk with exhilaration. For the first time in her life she was making an important moral decision on her own. For the first time—perhaps it would be the only time—she was veering away from her family's careful plans for her. What awaited her, good or evil, she had no idea. But for once, it would be hers. For three weeks. Maybe even longer.

"I'll tell you one thing, Willard," she said, trying to sound confident, "if Mitch Carey tries to use or cheat Roscoe, I'll personally slap a fraud charge on him that'll put him out of the music business. And I'll sue him for damages."

"Then I devoutly hope Mr. Carey behaves." Willard grinned. "He doesn't know he's got a little golden tigress coming after him."

"I'm hardly a tigress," Dinah protested, embarrassed.

"Yes, you are," Willard said, keeping his arm around her. "A tiny tigress who's afraid of mice, but a tigress, nonetheless. You just don't know it yet. Let's go join the picnic. We'll tell Vesta first, and then Roscoe."

She blushed slightly. Willard knew her terrible and humiliating secret. She had a mortal fear of mice. It was the only phobia she had, but it seemed an antiquated and totally shameful one. Being reminded of it, she didn't feel in the least like a tigress.

She was sure of only one thing. She had given her promise and now her duty would be to watch Mitch Carey as closely as if he were Satan. If he schemed for Roscoe's innocent and giddy soul, she would fight him to her last breath. She might not have accomplished much in Kakexia, but this much she could do—protect one vulnerable boy.

IN NASHVILLE, Mitch Carey sat at his battered desk. He was of medium height, but his lithe slimness and square shoulders made him seem taller. He radiated an aura of contained and slightly dangerous power. Also slightly dangerous was his dark Irish handsomeness. His thick hair with its pronounced widow's peak was black. Equally black were his eyebrows, which had a spectacularly roguish arch. His dark-lashed eyes were lazy lidded, making him look sensuous or bored or as if he were quietly plotting something both pleasurable and devious. Although few people have eyes that are truly green, Mitch Carey did; they were the pure light green eyes that reminded many of a panther's.

Carey's face could convey an extraordinary range of emotion. When he chose to use it, the wattage of his white smile could tumble birds out of trees. Right now he was looking from beneath his lazy lids with vaguely cloaked dislike because the object of his green gaze was Lucky Bucky Williston.

Lucky Bucky wore a snow-white cowboy suit. Its coat was embroidered with spangled wagon wheels in red, blue and green, and alligator boots. His blue Stetson had a band made of the skin of poisonous lizards. His huge thighs were crossed comfortably, and he had his feet on Mitch Carey's desk.

"So," said Lucky Bucky, a sly smile on his fat face, "you gonna get him? The hillbilly kid? Roscoe Hockenberry?"

"I'll get him, all right," Mitch Carey said. "He'd better be as good as you say. I've gone to a lot of trouble."

Lucky Bucky seemed to bloat slightly, as if offended. "Listen," he said importantly, "he's got it all. He's a little freaky, and stupid as a dog. But that's to our advantage. And when he sings, he's going to knock your socks off."

The corners of Carey's mouth turned down. His lids grew slightly more hooded. "I don't wear socks," he said in a slightly contemptuous voice. And he didn't. If Lucky Bucky were decked out as an oversize rhinestone cowboy, Mitch Carey was all upper-class casual, sockless, wearing expensive boating moccasins, form-fitting chino slacks and a dark blue polo shirt imported from Europe.

He yawned slightly, just to make Lucky Bucky nervous. "And get your feet off my desk, Williston," he added.

Lucky Bucky complied instantly, which took some complicated shifting of his weighty body.

"Well," Lucky Bucky said, adjusting his brilliant jacket as he tried to sound businesslike. "Who's gonna bring the kid? His mother?"

"His mother wouldn't last a day in Nashville," Carey replied sardonically. "She'd die of fright the first time she saw a tour bus. They're trying to talk some woman—a schoolteacher—into bringing him."

"A schoolteacher?" Lucky Bucky said with distaste. "What are we supposed to do with a schoolteacher? She'll try to stick her nose into everything. Think she knows it all."

Mitch yawned again, stretching his arms languidly. "Don't worry about the teacher," he murmured with almost insolent confidence. "I'll handle her. Personally. She's not going to stand in my way."

Lucky Bucky gave his employer a suspicious look. He had no doubts that Carey would handle the schoolteacher. Carey, for all his seeming indolence, was a frightening man, to Lucky Bucky's mind. He wasn't like his brother, Bobby, at all. Bobby Carey had been all wild enthusiasm and hectic action. He had come plunging into Nashville, bought the controlling interest in Diamond Horseshoe and taken Lucky Bucky on as trusted confidant and guiding force.

Bobby hadn't struck Lucky Bucky as a man with a good deal of sense, but he did have a good deal of money and a complete, if misplaced, trust in Lucky Bucky. Then the fun-loving fool went down to an untimely death in a small plane, and Mitch had appeared on the scene.

Mitch Carey made Lucky Bucky uneasy. It was as if he never stopped thinking—ever. Something was always going on behind those startling green eyes. But just what, Lucky Bucky had no idea.

He wasn't even sure Carey was honest. He was doubtful anybody that smart could be honest. Bucky had the feeling that soon Mitch Carey was going to start moving and when he did, Nashville would never be the same. The Hockenberry boy, of course, caught up in Carey's schemes, would never be the same, either. As for the little school-teacher…Lucky Bucky shrugged. The woman didn't stand a chance once Carey got her in his power. No chance in the world.

CHAPTER TWO

THE NEXT FEW DAYS sped by frenetically for Dinah. She had to phone and explain the situation to her parents. Her father, a state Supreme Court judge, was a bit vague about everything, as usual. His mind was always happiest mulling over the laws of Connecticut, not keeping track of the comings and goings of his household. If Dinah wanted to extend her "social work" a bit, it was fine with him.

"But be careful," he warned. "Show business is full of sharks, Dinah. If you're suspicious about anything, check with a good lawyer. I'll see that you get the name of the best."

"I just wonder how Dennis will take this," her mother brooded. "We should be planning your wedding, Dinah. Don't tell me you want to postpone it. Dennis is a saint, but you shouldn't try his patience."

Dinah tried hard to sound saintly herself. "I have a duty to this boy, Mother. It's not fair for me to teach one year, then think I can spend the rest of my life enjoying the family money. I don't think that's the kind of attitude Great-grandfather meant to instill."

"Your great-grandfather knew the precise limits of charity," Mrs. MacNeil said rather icily. "You'll do far more good preparing to work for the museum than frittering away your time on one student who's already shown his academic inadequacy. You should come home and pick out your gown. There are showers to be given. Teas. Cocktail parties. Just how long do you intend to be gone?''

"Maybe just three weeks," Dinah hedged, knowing that Roscoe very well might get a contract that would keep him in Nashville indefinitely. "Maybe . . . a little longer."

"Well, Dennis will be adorable about it," her mother said acidly. "But his mother is going to be very upset. I'm upset myself. We've been looking forward to this wedding for years. And now you run off, playing den mother to this silly boy."

"Actually," her father mused from his extension in the den, "she may be morally, if not actually legally, obliged to render any of these students more time. The original bequest stipulated each heir donate a full year to public welfare. Dinah's spent only a school year—I realize we've been lax enforcing the year requirement on those who chose to teach, but technically—"

"Oh, technically!" said her mother wearily and gave up. No one was going to win an argument with the judge when he was contemplating the wonderful complexities of a technicality. She fired one parting shot, however, for Dinah's benefit. "If Dennis consents to this—and he will—I'm going to be very angry with him, too. That young man never thinks of himself. He's too good to be true."

When Dinah hung up, she felt as guilty as her mother intended. Her only consolation was that her mother might be angry with her, but she would never be angry with Dennis. She considered him too perfect.

And Dennis, true to form, was considerate and polite when she phoned, the very epitome of the civilized gentleman. "You must do what you think is right, Dinah," he said cheerfully. "Stay as long as you're needed."

"You're sure?" Dinah asked. Sometimes Dennis was almost too considerate. It would be nice, she thought perversely, if he stormed passionately that he had waited long enough for her. But then, Dennis was not the type to be either stormy or passionate.

"We'll have forever together," he bubbled happily. "What difference can a few weeks or months make?"

"Oh, none—none," Dinah protested miserably. She wondered why she couldn't be as cheerful and philosophical about all this as Dennis.

"Then not to worry your liddle biddy head," baby-talked Dennis. "I mean, Di-Di, we have all of *eternity* to be married."

"Of course," Dinah agreed numbly. She could visualize Dennis clearly and it simply made her feel guiltier. He was such a nice person, and it was certainly not his fault that he was—well—less than staggeringly exciting. He was small and blond, as she was, with tiny hands and feet that her mother said were the mark of a true gentleman. He had a round pale face with round pale eyes and a silky mustache so blond that it was almost white. He was already in graduate school at Yale and aspired to become a professor of stringed instruments, specializing in the harp. The harp would only be his hobby, because his life's work would be keeping track of the family's stocks and bonds. Dinah's mother marveled at how someone as rich as Dennis could also be so nice, so cultivated and so talented, as well.

Dennis must have sensed her discomfort, for he tactfully changed the subject. "I'm certainly keeping busy this week," he giggled lightly. "My fingers just ache! The orchestra is practicing all week." He chattered on with animation. Only at the end of their conversation did he become serious.

"Are you sure you can handle a teenage boy?" he asked, sounding somewhat troubled for the first time. "They can be animals. I remember Boy Scouts—uck. There was a big bully who always used to put toads in my sleeping bag, stuff me in and zip me up. I still have nightmares of horrid hopping feet pummeling me. It was the only time in my life I was ever truly tempted to tattle.''

"I can handle him," Dinah said.

"Well, if you say so, that's that," he answered agreeably. "But whatever you do, try to change his musical tastes, will you? I mean—country and western. Oh! That's one thing I'll never tell anyone. I'll have to say you're chaperoning a young cellist off to London or something." She could almost feel Dennis's shudder of genteel distaste through the phone line.

"That's snobbish, Dennis. Country music may not be to your taste, but a lot of people enjoy it." Dinah heard the sharpness in her retort and flinched, biting her lip. Dennis was going out of his way to be understanding and cheerful, and she had unaccountably become irritable with him. "I'm sorry," she said contritely.

"No, no, no," contradicted Dennis. "You're right. *I'm* sorry. The child can't help being underprivileged. It's so good of you to take on his humble hopes and dreams. Use as much time as you need, darling. I want only that you be happy. We can survive this little separation. We could survive a separation of years and years. Now imagine that I'm kissing you on your little lips. Then tell me you adore me."

"I—I—" stammered Dinah. She tried to say she loved him, but the words caught in her throat.

"Say it, darling," Dennis ordered benignly. "And think of the purity of our love. Remember that physical togetherness isn't everything. It's hardly anything, in fact."

"I—I can't," she gasped, almost panicking. "Somebody's at the door. They'll hear me. Goodbye, Dennis. You're a darling. I'll call you from Nashville."

Dinah hung up, emotionally exhausted. She felt confused and slightly traitorous. Since childhood Dennis had
been her most treasured companion. Her mother always
told her how lucky she was that Dennis was so devoted. Why
did she feel that going to Nashville was a way of escaping
from Dennis a bit longer? Why did she need to escape from
him?

The knocking on the screen door grew more insistent. She
went to answer, grateful for the distraction.

"Oh, hello, Roscoe," she said. Roscoe came to talk to her
each evening. He also checked her mousetraps. He was such
a good-hearted boy; he was the only one she could trust with
the job. She knew he would never embarrass her by telling
the other students. If he found a mouse, he was always
careful to never let her so much as glimpse it.

Now he stood shyly on the porch of the trailer she rented.
His old white T-shirt had been crudely lettered with the
name of his singing idol, Hank Williams. He was wearing
his too-large white cowboy hat and carrying his guitar.

"Hey," he said cheerfully. "Come out and set a spell before I check your mousetraps. I writ a new song. You'll like
it."

Dinah, wearing a sprigged print blouse and lavender cu-
lottes, gave him a fatigued smile, but went out to sit beside
him on the unpainted steps. She often found his songs foreign to her tastes but admired the way he produced them as
naturally as a healthy apple tree produced apples.

Roscoe pushed his big hat up because it kept sliding over
his eyes. He gave her a lopsided grin. A lower front tooth
was missing, and Dinah silently noted that she'd have to see
to getting it fixed in Nashville. That, and having his eyes
tested. She was sure Roscoe's eyes were weak, which might
have intensified his study problems.

"What have you written now?" she asked, smiling at him in spite of herself. He was such an innocent, likable boy. "I hope it's not another sad one." Most of Roscoe's songs were sad, which was one reason Dinah found his music unsettling.

"Naw," said Roscoe cheerfully. "This one's real happy." He looked at her, and his skinny face suddenly sobered. "You look like a sad song yourself. Is somethin' wrong? Has somethin' happened?"

"No, of course not," she said hastily. For all of Roscoe's giddiness, he was sometimes too perceptive. She looked away from him, out at the hills. Unconsciously she twisted the big ring on her finger.

"It's too tight, ain't it?" he asked confidentially.

"What?" she asked, startled. Then she realized she was fidgeting with the diamond and stopped. "No. It fits fine," she said with false cheerfulness.

"I didn't mean it was too tight on your fingers," Roscoe said, with wide-eyed sincerity. "I meant it's too tight on your life."

"Everybody who's getting married gets nervous," Dinah stated defensively. "When you're older, you'll understand."

"It don't sound right to me," replied Roscoe, and began tuning his guitar. "Know what? I think you need to go to Nashville as much as I do."

Dinah looked at him half in amusement and half in disbelief. "Whatever for?" she asked. "What could I possibly need in Nashville?"

But Roscoe only grinned his crooked grin and started singing a love song.

Dinah leaned back against the porch railing and listened, watching the sunset. She was filled with a strange and trou-

bling restlessness. Time was all she needed, she told herself.
Time.

TIME VANISHED. It seemed to Dinah that one moment she
had been sitting on the shabby little porch in Kakexia, with
Roscoe singing, and the next moment she was sitting on the
edge of a giant heart-shaped bed in an enormous bedroom
in an even more enormous mansion in Nashville.

Wrong, Dinah amended nervously, this wasn't a bedroom, it was a *boudoir*, so blatantly sensuous that it was
intimidating. The heart-shaped bed not only had a scarlet
satin coverlet edged lushly with lace, it had a canopy, also
heart shaped, lined with the same blinding red satin and
curtained with the same extravagance of lace.

The carpet was thick and white, scattered with large heart-
shaped rugs of fake white fur. The rest of the furniture was
white-and-gold French provincial. Dinah's trained eye knew
it was imitation, and gaudy imitation at that.

The huge windows were draped in blood-red satin and
held back with elaborate gold ties. Among the paintings on
the walls, she counted five portraying nymphs frolicking
with satyrs. They were so full of extraneous and libidinous
detail that they made her dizzy.

She rose and tried looking out the tall windows, but that
only made her dizzier. It was evening in Nashville, and her
view was of a swimming pool and a formal garden. But the
swimming pool, Dinah noted with disbelief, was shaped like
a guitar and lined with gold tiles. The lovely flowers were
planted in plots that resembled musical objects: banjos, pi-
anos, musical notes, staffs and clef signs. She pulled the
blinds and turned away with a shudder.

She had a private bath whose luxury she found almost
humiliating. The sunken Jacuzzi was colored a florid pink

and shaped like a heart. Its golden faucets had huge false rubies imbedded in them.

She sank back, dazed, on the bed again. The room, like the little she had seen of the house, was ostentatious beyond belief.

Still bone tired by the tedious flight to Nashville, boggled by the mansion and her unspeakable room, she dreaded meeting Mitch Carey. So far she had encountered his chauffeur, housekeeper and a pair of giggling maids with beehive hairdos. Everyone had been so friendly that Dinah was thrown even further off guard. Servants in Connecticut didn't say things like, "Hi, y'all. Make yourselves at home, you hear."

One of the giggling maids had installed her in this bordellolike room, telling her to rest and freshen up, that Mr. Carey would see her at about eight.

Dinah sat numbly on the edge of the bed. She didn't have energy to change her clothes. She wore a long-sleeved, high-necked dress, demurely striped with misty blue-gray, her tiny waist accentuated by the dark blue belt. She looked like a small Victorian missionary somehow trapped in the opulence of the boudoir.

Absently she picked up a gold-and-ivory music box, an obviously expensive antique. She opened its ornate lid and winced when it played some sort of honky-tonk country tune. Somebody, Mitch Carey, most likely, had actually rigged the beautiful piece to play country music.

We have fallen in among madmen, Dinah thought dismally. In Connecticut, her family lived in a mansion, but it was tasteful, understated to the point of modesty. Her father believed one should enjoy one's wealth, but within decorous limits—it was never to be flaunted.

Roscoe, she feared, would be mightily impressed by this display. Her only comfort was that between the plane ride

and his excitement, he had turned so many shades of nau-
seated green that he had been able to do little but be led
staggering off to a room of his own. Dinah hoped his ex-
haustion had finally forced him to sleep. The boy was liter-
ally sick with nerves. So, for that matter, was Dinah.

Drat Mitch Carey, drat his offers, and drat his vile pal-
ace of pleasures, she thought. Ineffectually she struck a
heart-shaped pillow with her small fist. How could she deal
with a man who lived in the midst of such crude spectacle?
He had the tastes of a savage, and probably the morals to
match.

Just then the gold-and-jeweled phone on her night table
jingled. She picked it up as gingerly as if she expected to
hear the devil himself inviting her to step downstairs and
sign Roscoe's—and her own—fate over to him in blood.

"Hello," she said in her most dignified tone, but her heart
rattled madly in her chest.

"Miss MacNeil. Mitchell Carey here. I hope your flight
was pleasant." The voice made Dinah sit up straight and her
heart hammer more erratically. It was as soft, deep and slow
as the satisfied purr of a jungle cat. It had not the faintest
trace of the Southern accent she had grown accustomed to
in the past months. It was also a voice that implied imme-
diate intimacy.

Dinah's mouth went dry. "The trip was fine—long, but
fine."

"I'm sorry air travel didn't agree with Roscoe," he said
in the same slow and velvety tone. "I've left word that he
not be disturbed."

"It wasn't just the flight," Dinah explained, still stunned
by the provocative timbre of Mitch Carey's voice. "His
mother said she didn't think he slept at all the past two
nights. And he's been too nervous to eat. This is all a rather
overwhelming experience for him, Mr. Carey."

"I'm sure," Mitch replied smoothly. "But I hope your metabolism has fared better. I was wondering if you'd care to join me on the patio for a quiet supper. We need to talk. We're going to have to get to know each other."

Good heavens, thought Dinah in mild panic. The man's simplest statement was as titillating as the rustle of silken sheets.

"My metabolism is even enough," she replied crisply, though the statement wasn't altogether true. "I could do with some supper. And yes, we do need to get to know each other. We're going to have to deal with each other frankly, Mr. Carey. My only purpose here is to protect Roscoe's interests."

There was a pause, only as long as a pulse. "I like a frank woman, Miss MacNeil," he drawled. "And one with a healthy metabolism. Can you find your way to the patio? Or shall I send someone to escort you?"

Dinah would have liked to say she'd make her way to the patio alone, but in truth, the mansion was vast, and its unrelenting garishness had totally disoriented her. "I suppose you should send someone," she admitted.

"Fine," replied the jungle purr. "There'll be a knock on your door in ten minutes. Is that too soon?"

"Ten minutes will be quite adequate," she replied stiffly.

"Wonderful," he breathed. "I look forward to meeting you, Miss MacNeil." He hung up before she could gather her wits to say goodbye.

Dinah sat motionless on the big gaudy bed. Her heart kept on beating like some mad drum trying to send her a message of enormous importance.

Precisely ten minutes after she had hung up the phone, Dinah heard a brisk rapping at her door. She marched across the white carpet and opened the door, expecting one of the giggling maids.

Instead a man lounged against the sill. He wore expensive casual white pleated trousers, an off-white short-sleeved pullover, tassled moccasins and no socks. He was at least eight inches taller than Dinah, who stood five foot in her blue pumps.

He was bronzed and dark-haired, with a devastatingly attractive white smile and a cleft in his chin. About thirty-three, he looked as clean-cut and trim as a tennis pro. His easy stance and smile made him seem friendly, unpretentious and nonchalant.

Hello! Dinah thought, surprised again—who's this? He didn't fit her picture of anyone connected to the country music business. All she could think of was secretary. This pleasant and sporty man must have been Mitch Carey's secretary—the man who took care of all the little business details for him—such as adding, subtracting and spelling.

But then she noticed the almost devilish arch of his black brows and the glitter in his cat-green eyes. Oh, no, she thought in disbelief. When he spoke, the smooth, almost taunting slowness of his voice put an end to any doubt.

"*Bon soir,* Miss MacNeil. I thought it would be friendlier if I fetched you myself. I hope you don't mind that I didn't dress for supper. I like to keep things low-key."

It was Mitch Carey, no mistake. He straightened, gave her that blazing white smile again and offered her his arm. "Shall we?" he asked, and his left brow managed to take on a particularly wicked crook.

"Certainly," she managed to say, and as if there was no choice, she laced her arm through his proffered one. As her bare hand touched the sun-gilded hardness of his muscles, she felt so odd that it almost made her faint. She knew he was fully aware of how much he had taken her by surprise. She could think of nothing at all to say as he walked her down the hall to the curving staircase.

"You're very quiet," he observed, patting her hand companionably. "Still tired from your trip? I hope I don't presume in asking you to join me this evening."

The touch of his hand on hers turned her nerves into bundles of fire. "You're not what I expected," she said bluntly. *Honesty is the best policy,* she thought desperately.

He gave her a lazy smile as they started down the spiral staircase. "Just what did you expect?"

Dinah gestured helplessly with her free hand, indicating the overdone grandeur around them. "Somebody who matched the surroundings," she said nervously, wondering if he'd be offended.

He shrugged, cast a contemptuous glance at the chandeliers, the false marble of the stairs. "Oh," he said dismissively. "This. A bit overdone, isn't it?"

"Well—" Dinah said, embarrassed, then swallowed hard.

"Overdone—especially to someone like you," he insisted, nodding seriously. "Fortunately, it isn't mine. I'm just finishing up a year's lease on it. It belongs to a star on a year's world tour. In the meantime, I have to live somewhere."

"Of course," Dinah said, then realized what a stupid and inadequate response it was. She fought to recover her wits. She was already ill armed to take on Nashville. She couldn't afford to be put any more off balance just because a stranger happened to be not merely handsome but strangely electrifying, as well.

"Why lease this house, though?" she asked. "To impress your clients?"

He gave another elegant shrug. "Some are impressed. Some aren't. I didn't lease it myself—I sort of inherited the lease."

They had reached the bottom of the stairs and crossed a huge foyer where a fountain played, splashing loudly. Water issued in a crystal stream, spewed from the mouth of some sort of marble fish that looked like a particularly ugly carp.

"Just how did you inherit it?" Dinah asked suspiciously. Now that her initial shock had subsided, she knew she must be on guard against this man. He seemed unstudied, almost lackadaisical, but instinct told her he was an adversary far more formidable than any she had anticipated.

"How'd I inherit it?" he asked offhandedly. He escorted her across the wide court of a sun room cluttered with exotic plants. "The usual way. Somebody died. But let's discuss more pleasant subjects. Or at least more neutral ones. Do you like lobster?"

Dinah sensed a disturbing mockery beneath his words. "Lobster is fine," she said, wishing he would remove his arm from hers. It felt altogether too proprietary.

He opened the door of the sun room and ushered her onto a huge patio. An ornate table, its lace cloth billowing in the evening breeze, was before them, fully set. Candles in silver holders had flames that danced, and a simple arrangement of white roses in a silver bowl served as a centerpiece.

Mitch Carey pulled out a chair for her, and she sank into it gratefully, her knees weak. The patio was immense, edged with blooming roses, and marred only by another of those horrid spouting carp statues at the far end.

"I took the liberty of ordering champagne," he said, as a white-coated man with a bushy beard suddenly appeared to uncork a bottle of Dom Perignon. "I think the arrival of you—and your protégé, Roscoe—calls for it."

"Roscoe isn't my protégé." She kept her voice polite but cool. "He's yours. At least, so it would seem." She watched the servant pour the foaming champagne.

"You seem dubious," Mitch challenged silkily. He held his champagne flute out to her in a toast. "Here's to trust. May it grow and flourish between us."

"May it indeed," Dinah answered evenly, touching her glass lightly against his.

He took a small sip. Dinah took a deep one to quiet her dancing nerves. He studied her in silence over the rim of his glass. His half-lowered lids seemed almost indolent, but his pale emerald gaze was disconcertingly intent.

"I have a feeling," he murmured, "that right now you don't trust me at all. Correct?"

Dinah paused. She returned a look as intent as his. "Correct," she said at last. "I told you, you're not what I expected. And I don't know what you want with Roscoe. Would you care to explain?"

He smiled slightly. "Maybe you shouldn't have had any expectations. Preconceptions are dangerous—especially in a place like Nashville. As for what I want with Roscoe—it's simple: his talent. He and I can both profit from it."

She took another sip of champagne. "That's easy to say," she replied evenly. "It's what you're expected to say. But you know nothing about him."

His smile didn't waver. "I have Lucky Bucky Williston's report. I've heard the tapes. And I have another friend who's heard Roscoe. That report was even more glowing than Bucky's."

"Who?" Dinah asked skeptically. She knew of nobody in Nashville who'd had direct contact with Roscoe except for Lucky Bucky.

Mitch's eyes still hadn't left hers. She wasn't sure if he was waging a war of nerves, beginning a seduction or both.

"My friend's name would probably mean nothing to you," he replied with a slight cock of his head. "Lucky Bucky can smell talent the way a shark smells blood. But my friend—my friend is practically infallible when it comes to spotting not merely talent, but genius. What do I need to know about Roscoe except that?''

Dinah squared her shoulders. The slightly devilish smile of the man, his perfect and intimidating self-possession kept her both wary and vaguely excited.

"You should know," she parried, "that 'genius' is a term thrown around far too loosely. Roscoe is just a boy who likes to sing. He's naive, even innocent. He hasn't got a sophisticated bone in his body. You, on the other hand, Mr. Carey, seem to have a great deal of sophistication. Which puts Roscoe at a disadvantage."

"Perhaps, Miss MacNeil," Mitch countered, raising his glass to her in tribute, "you have enough sophistication for both the boy and yourself. You're not what I would have expected, either—of a schoolteacher from Kakexia, Kentucky."

"Maybe preconceptions are dangerous about a place like Kakexia, too," Dinah returned coolly. "Or about schoolteachers."

If he found her answer tart, he wasn't fazed. He only raised a brow in slight amusement. "But when the little teacher from Kentucky is none other Dinah Windsor MacNeil, the sophistication isn't surprising. That's who you are, isn't it?" His smile was almost smug. "Daughter of Judge Stuart MacNeil? Niece of the former Governor Kirk MacNeil? And of course, great-granddaughter of noted steel magnate and philanthropist Andrew Gilmore MacNeil?"

Dinah kept from sputtering on a mouthful of champagne. She was grateful for the distraction of the waiter, who was setting down a small silver tray of shrimp.

She managed to recover quickly. "As a teacher I congratulate you," she remarked. "You've done your homework."

"Willard Wakefield hinted as much about you," Mitch returned, one side of his mouth still curled in a maddening smile. "I had someone else do the homework. Amusing, eh? One of the august MacNeils suddenly plunged into the middle of Nashville managing a hillbilly singer."

He gazed up at the darkening sky. His quirked brow gave him a thoughtful air. "I like it," he muttered, almost to himself. "It has infinite publicity possibilities. 'Socialite joins the honky-tonk guitar set. Former debutante guides career of country singer.'"

Dinah carefully set down the shrimp she had speared. She glared formidably at Mitch, but he remained impervious. "You keep my name out of this," she ordered. "I came here to make sure you didn't exploit Roscoe, and I guarantee that you won't exploit me. Don't dare even think of it."

His expression became cool, almost bored. "I've always dared exactly what I please, Miss MacNeil."

"Then," she said, leaning closer to him across the table, trying to make her anger register, "suppose you dare tell me exactly what it is you intend to do for Roscoe? All your 'offers,' all your 'generosity,' have been a little too good to be true. What do you want from him?"

He sighed, as if the conversation wearied him. "I told you. His talent—if it's as great as my sources indicate. In return for his talent, he'll be reimbursed. Handsomely. And fairly. I guarantee that."

"Very pretty—if true," Dinah replied, raising her chin.

"It's true. He has raw ability. I'm willing to spend money to refine it."

"And out of it, precisely what do you get?" she challenged. "Not mere satisfaction, I assume. A large cut of the profits, I'm certain."

"Satisfaction, yes. Profits, again, my fair share only."

Dinah shook her head in disbelief. "You're willing to spend this time, this effort, and this money—and you expect only a fair and modest share? That's all?"

He gave a small laugh. "Not quite all." He smiled, and something in his smile frightened her.

"What else, then?" she demanded.

He stared at her, his face a mocking mask. "It's simple," he said at last. "I want his soul."

Dinah stared at him in dismay. She wasn't certain that he was joking. "Well," she said quietly, her expression one of determination, "Roscoe's soul was one of the things I was sent here to protect."

He gave her his most disarming smile, then picked up her hand and planted a warm and lingering kiss on her knuckles. She was too stunned to object.

"Then, my dear Miss MacNeil," he offered in a voice as soft as silk, "I suppose I'll have to get your soul first."

"Are you mad?" she asked, aghast. She tried to draw her hand away, but his clasp was firm.

He stared down at her engagement ring, which sparkled in the candlelight. "No," he said, not smiling for once. "I'm perfectly sane. But the man who put this on your finger—" he shifted her hand slightly, so that the large diamond caught fire in the dancing light "—and then let you go—that man is mad."

"Don't be impertinent!" Dinah breathed hotly. She wished he would release her hand. And yet his touch sent a warm current dancing through her body.

"My dear," he cautioned, "I was born impertinent. Just as you were born proud. And Roscoe was born gifted. It has the makings of a fascinating combination."

CHAPTER THREE

HE KISSED her hand again, lightly yet lingeringly, then released it. She snatched it back as if from a dangerous beast. She wondered if she should simply flee, leaving him sitting in the wavering candlelight and the gathering darkness.

"Oh, calm down. No offense was meant," he commanded with a change of tone so sudden that she was again caught off guard. He glanced idly at her heaving breasts then off to the fireflies that winked among the shrubs. "Let's get back to Roscoe. He's what's important. We've got business to discuss. Stop looking like an affronted princess and eat."

The servant, who was huge yet moved as softly as a shadow, set chilled crystal bowls of Caesar salad before them. Dinah nervously drained her glass of champagne and when she set it down, Mitch automatically refilled it.

He picked up his salad fork. It seemed to wink in the candlelight. "Tell me more about Roscoe," he said dispassionately.

Self-consciously, she rubbed her hand where his lips had brushed it. She was surprised his kiss hadn't left a mark that glowed in the dark. Her skin still felt prickly.

"Roscoe's one of the most natural, unaffected people I've ever known," she said crisply. "But he needs someone to watch out for him."

"Naturally," Mitch said with a shrug. "Otherwise you wouldn't be here."

"Most men in his family worked in the mines. But one uncle went to Pennsylvania to work in a box factory. When Roscoe was eleven, his father decided to do the same. He packed the family up and took them to Philadelphia. There were seven children: an elder brother and sister, Roscoe and four younger sisters."

"The move didn't work out, obviously," commented Mitch wryly.

Dinah shook her head. "From what Roscoe's mother, Vesta, says, it was a disastrous two years. She hated the city and could never cope with it. And all the stories about plentiful jobs and the streets being paved with gold were just that—stories. They came home to Kakexia."

"And just what did Roscoe do during these two years among the golden streets of Philadelphia?" he asked. But the gold Mitch Carey seemed interested in was that of her hair, fluttering softly in the warm breeze.

Dinah tried to ignore the way he was making her skin tingle. "Mostly, as they say in the hills, he pined. He was homesick. It's the period when his real troubles with his studies started. Vesta said children at school made fun of his Southern accent, and his teacher ridiculed him. Academically, he never really recovered. I'm sure he's got some vision problems, too. I want to check it out. But Philadelphia put him completely off stride."

"Culture shock, eh?" Mitch offered. He was leaning his chin on his fist, still watching the wind play with her gleaming locks.

"His only outlet was his guitar. He laughs about it now, but he says he was so miserable that all he liked to do was shut himself up in the bathroom, play his guitar and see how many ways he could make his voice bounce off the tile."

"In short," Mitch smiled, "he reinvented the echo chamber of the recording studio."

Dinah ran a hand over her fluttering hair self-consciously. The man was irritating and provocative at the same time. He hardly seemed to be listening to her words, simply staring, for no apparent reason, at the play of her hair about her face.

"I suppose he did," she said shortly. "At any rate, Roscoe was thirteen when they went back to Kakexia. When he was fourteen, one of the mines had a cave-in. Nine men died. Three of them were in Roscoe's family—his father, his brother and one of his uncles."

Mitch's green gaze suddenly left her hair and looked into the depths of her sapphire eyes. "Most dangerous job in the world, you know," he said, with no expression.

"What?" she said, startled by the intensity of his stare and the flatness of his voice.

"Mining," he answered indifferently. "Most dangerous job in the world. Do you know what the second most dangerous is?"

"On some days, I'd say it was teaching," she replied, wondering if he would smile.

He didn't. "Wrong," he said. "The music business."

The servant removed the salad plates, then appeared with platters of lobster thermidor and a steaming silver bowl of rice with almonds. Dinah was grateful for the distraction.

By the time the man disappeared into the house, Dinah felt her self-possession returning. For one thing, Mitch Carey had moved his musing scrutiny from her to his lobster.

"I don't doubt that the music business is dangerous, Mr. Carey," she asserted. "That's why I'm not amused when you say you want Roscoe's soul. Roscoe's soul will stay his own—as long as I'm around to say anything about it."

He arched one black brow. "Then you'd better stay around a long time. Temptations never end." He looked up long enough to give her a brief but dazzling smile.

"It's not a joking matter," she protested.

"I'm not joking."

"Then precisely what are you doing?" she demanded.

"Oh," he muttered, raising one squared shoulder slightly. "Watching your reactions, mostly."

She set down her fork. She felt her face burn with a combination of frustration and anger.

"Now, now," he said, and flashed another fleeting smile before returning his attention to his lobster.

"Why don't you watch me react to a few straight answers?" she returned with spirit. "First, what exactly are your qualifications to run a record company? Second, how reputable is Diamond Horseshoe? And third, precisely what are you prepared to offer Roscoe, and what does he get from you in return?"

"Would you pass the salt, please?"

Dinah picked up the silver shaker, which he could have reached himself, and set it down in front of him with a resounding thump.

He smiled. "Thanks," he said, mockery dripping from his voice.

She pushed her platter away and crossed her arms over her breasts. She stared at him in challenge. "Well?" she demanded.

He paused a moment, savoring his lobster. His black brows lifted eloquently. "What are my qualifications to produce records? Lots of people would tell you in one word— None. I've never actually done this before."

"What?" she said very quietly.

"None," he repeated cheerfully, ignoring the coldness in her tone. "And anyone will tell you the reputation of Diamond Horseshoe Records—it's terrible."

"Let me get this straight," Dinah said, narrowing her eyes at the nonchalant figure across the candlelit table. "Your company has a terrible reputation, and you aren't qualified to run it. Correct?"

He scratched the cleft in his chin. He gazed thoughtfully off into the darkness. "Yes and no," he replied. "I've been in Nashville only two months. People say I'm not qualified because they don't know me. They look down on Diamond Horseshoe because I haven't transformed it yet."

"Brave words," Dinah said sarcastically. "Why did you get yourself in this position? Why buy a bad company? Why not buy a good one, if you're so bright, or start one yourself?"

"I didn't buy it," he explained. He gestured casually toward the mansion. "It's like the house. I inherited it."

"You—" she paused for ironic effect "—inherited it. May I ask from whom?"

"Certainly," he answered. "From my brother. He fancied himself a great entrepreneur. He also liked to think of himself as a down-to-earth, back-to-basics kind of fellow. Hence, he attempted to combine the two and become a magnate of country music."

Dinah looked at him in amazement, but the man was completely unflappable.

"Why," she asked with great deliberateness, "did your brother have a terrible company?"

He looked up as if she had asked him the most obvious of questions. "Oh," he said, then gave a rueful half smile. "He was something of an idiot."

"Mr. Carey!" she cried. She crumpled her napkin and threw it down next to her silverware.

He looked at her innocently. "What's wrong?"

She was breathing hard again. "Your own brother died—recently, I assume—and you're calling him an idiot? How callous!"

He put his hands out in a placating motion. "I'm not speaking ill of the dead," he said guilelessly. "I'm speaking the truth of the dead. Bobby could be idiotic. He never thought things through. He was impulsive, reckless and, basically, self-destructive. Ask anybody who knew him. It's sad, but true."

"It's still not very nice to say," Dinah objected, for as a MacNeil, she was bred to take family loyalty as a sacred duty.

His tone grew more serious. He leaned toward her slightly. Challenge played in his cat-green eyes. "You wanted honesty. So don't object to it. Tell me, would a sensible man lease a house like this?"

He looked significantly at the ugly fountain, where the marble carp continued to spit water at the starlight. She swallowed hard, remembering her room with its red heart-shaped bed, its gallery of satyrs and pursuing nymphs.

"I put you in that room for a reason," he said, as if reading her mind. "So you could see the worst of this place and understand. Surely, somewhere in your impeccable pedigree, you can find a relative you think is an idiot."

Dinah sat stonily, gazing at her napkin. She had to admit, if she were honest, she did think her cousin Dougal was impossible. He was worse than impossible. He was the most insensitive person she knew, and his childish pranks had left lasting psychological scars on her.

Mitch was right. Dougal was odious and she did consider him an idiot. She smiled shyly at Mitch. He smiled back. His irreverent honesty had disarmed her. For a moment it seemed the most pleasant and natural thing in the world to smile with him.

Then his eyes rested on her lips, and the night became charged with heat, expectation and a sense of the darkness suddenly coming to life.

"Ah," he said softly. And she knew he wasn't smiling because he had caught her thinking of Dougal. He had caught her becoming altogether too conscious of him.

"Still," she said, shaking her head in the hopes she'd find some clarity still intact, "you don't have to be so brutally frank, do you? Aren't you sorry your brother died?"

His face grew serious, the green eyes hooded. "I miss him. I wish somebody could have saved him. I wish to hell I could have saved him. He didn't want any help from me. He wanted to show the world he could do things on his own. If I'd had longer, maybe I could have talked sense into him, but time ran out. So all I can save is the one decent idea he ever had in his life—Diamond Horseshoe. And I suppose he would have wanted me to, or he wouldn't have left it to me."

Dinah spread her napkin on her lap again and pretended to focus her attention on smoothing it out. "What makes you think Diamond Horseshoe is a good idea?" she probed. "And what makes you think you can save it?"

He signaled for more champagne, and when it arrived, refilled both glasses. "Instinct tells me it's a good idea," he said confidently. "I can make it work because I'm organized and disciplined. I can also make it work because of Roscoe—if he can deliver what I want."

She slipped him a sideways glance. "You're going to build a small empire on Roscoe? A sixteen-year-old boy? Perhaps your instincts aren't as infallible as you think."

She gave him a tight, falsely sweet smile to show him she was ready to put him in the same category as he had put his late brother—slightly crazed.

"No," he purred in his lazy voice. "Not a small empire. A large one. And not just on Roscoe. On a stable of the best talent in the industry."

"And what does Roscoe get?" she confronted him. "For helping you become the emperor of Nashville?"

He leaned his chin on his fist, and once more began his disconcerting trick of watching her blond hair stir around her face in the candlelight. "First, he gets the most valuable commodity in show business, the pearl beyond price. He gets a break."

"A break," she said sardonically. "How delightful. That won't be much to send back to his mother and sisters, will it? Your generosity overwhelms."

His eyes drifted back to hers. They were cold as pale green ice. "I don't have him under contract yet, Miss MacNeil. Do you want a week to take him all over Music City trying to find him a break somewhere else? You're perfectly welcome. You'll slink back here with your tongue out after you've hit those streets awhile. You'll kiss the hem of my garment for such a break."

Dinah fought hard to keep from choking on her lobster. "I'd rather die, Mr. Carey, than even contemplate kissing the hem of your garment. And I just may look somewhere else. If he has as much talent as you think, perhaps I shouldn't let him take the first offer that comes along, especially when the offer is from the admittedly unqualified director of a substandard company."

"Umm," he said, watching the bubbles rise in his glass. "Spoken like a true Scot. I'm offering Roscoe more than a break, of course. I'll treat him fairly and decently. I'll try to get the best people involved with his development."

"More easily promised than delivered," Dinah replied coolly. "And maybe you're bluffing. Maybe I could go out and find Roscoe something more promising. After all, Mr.

Carey, so far all you have on your business ledger are dreams. A week, you say? I'll take it."

His expression was one of mocking admiration. "I see in you the courage and determination that allowed your great-grandfather to get off the boat as a penniless boy and rise to become one of the richest men in the nation—the epitome of the American Dream. I also see the old boy's fabled arrogance. Blood does tell—sometimes."

"We'll see if it does," Dinah answered stiffly.

"But you and Roscoe will, of course, stay here, as agreed," he continued smoothly. "I'll pay for your daily expenses and put a car at your disposal. But in the meantime, I insist on being able to work with Roscoe myself. I want a short time with him each day, if we can manage. Just to get to know him."

He signaled to the servant, who materialized instantly with a thick sheaf of papers. Mitch took them and handed them to her. The waiter disappeared again, as if he were a genie. "If you haven't found anything better by the end of one week, you may consider this," he said, sounding almost bored again. "It's the contract I may offer Roscoe. Look it over. See what you think."

She opened her large blue straw purse and thrust the papers inside without looking at them. "I'll read them when I can give them my full attention."

The corner of his mouth curled slightly. "In that stylish purse," he murmured silkily, "I'd guess you have a piece of paper with the name of the best lawyer in Nashville. The better to check me out."

Dinah blinked hard. The man really did seem clairvoyant sometimes. She said nothing.

"And," he went on, contemplating his champagne bubbles again, "I'd wager money on what that name is."

She kept her silence. She stared at him in challenge. Her father had advised her about whom to consult, and the names were written down and tucked inside her wallet.

The servant came to clear their plates away. He set down a big helping of chocolate mousse for each of them. Mitch looked at her with perfect self-assurance. "The name within your purse is—let's see." He stared for a moment up at the stars, as if deep in thought. "Roman Hornsby III. Correct? And a MacNeil, reputedly canny conservative, would always have a spare, just in case. So the name of the second lawyer you have is Richard Ortison. Right?"

Dinah's blue eyes widened in bewildered apprehension. He was correct. Those were the very names her father had given her.

"Take the contract to either." Mitch practically yawned. "Take it to both. They'll tell you it's more than fair."

Disquieted, Dinah toyed with the mousse, no longer hungry. Perhaps he was bluffing again, trying by a show of brashness to keep her from consulting either lawyer.

He reached into his back pocket and drew out a small square of paper. "I said I'd see Roscoe had the best possible people to work with," he informed her. "Ask anybody in Nashville about these recommendations. The people I've listed here are young, but extremely talented. They may be willing to work with the boy. As for me, check me out. Any way you choose."

"I intend to," she answered grimly. She put the folded paper in her purse with the contract, then stared dejectedly at her mousse. If Mitch Carey was a charlatan, he was as bold as they came.

He saw her pensiveness and lack of appetite and pushed his dessert away, half-eaten. "Coffee?" he asked with the utmost politeness. "A liqueur, perhaps?"

"Nothing," Dinah answered shortly. She was deep in thought, thought liberally laced with worry. Perhaps she had taken on more than she could handle.

"You look tired," he said gently. "I'll take you back to your room."

She started to object, but he insisted. "This house is a maze. It's ridiculously big. I'll help you find your way."

Then he was on his feet, helping her from her chair. This time she resisted, a bit too much, perhaps, when he offered to take her arm. The candles were guttering now, their light inconstant. But the stars were bright and the moon half-full.

He stared down at her with an air of authority. He put his hands out, gripping her upper arms firmly. "No," he breathed. "Don't fight me. Don't refuse a helping hand—or arm—when it's offered. I said I'd help you find your way. I will. Through this house. And through Nashville."

His face was shadowed and she could not read it. But she could feel the unwarranted coursing of blood through her body at his touch, his nearness, and his cool, whispery voice. She sucked in her breath.

In spite of everything sense told her, Dinah felt shaken by this unpredictable man. His air of command was absolute, yet so casual it was as if he were not an ordinary mortal but a king, traveling in disguise, yet never forgetting he was king.

He was casting a spell over her, she realized, an extremely potent and irresistible one. *Because,* she realized with sudden insight, *he'll stop at nothing to get what he wants, and I don't even really understand what he wants.*

She willed her body to go nerveless, her flesh and muscles to chill. "And for all this wonderful help and guidance," she uttered between clenched teeth, "all you ask is our souls—Roscoe's and mine."

His hands fell away, he stepped back slightly, but this time when he took her arm, she didn't dare resist. "No," he corrected. "Simply your loyalty."

He walked her through the shadows back toward the sun room, which was now dark except for the starlight and moonlight that fell through the many windows. *Loyalty?* she thought distrustfully. *But hadn't he said he wanted their souls?*

"Loyalty," he repeated, although she had said nothing. "I treat my people well, and in return I demand loyalty. Because without loyalty I can build nothing. And I intend to build a great deal."

She was grateful when they reached the lights of the overdecorated foyer. She had a sudden and irrational urge to escape. The dark, lean man who towered beside her was too close, too disturbing.

They ascended the curving stairs in silence. He walked her to her door. He released her arm and stood staring down at her, his mouth curved in its indolent smile. "Try to get a good night's sleep," he advised. "You have one week to come up with a better offer than mine for Roscoe. It's going to be tiring—and disappointing."

She tilted her chin up at him in defiance. "You may be trying to bluff me."

"You're seriously underestimating me, Miss MacNeil," he answered easily. "Never underestimate anything in Nashville. It's a city of surprises."

Dinah could feel an unsettling current growing between them, but she refused to flinch. "You never told me why you think you can make Diamond Horseshoe into a success. Or Roscoe with it," she reminded him. "Just what is your background? What did you do before this?"

His unsettling smile intensified the current leaping between them. "Before this? Some would claim I never worked a day in my life. I, of course, look at it differently."

Again her equilibrium tumbled away and disappeared. "But—" she began in dismay.

He cut her off by taking her in his arms. "And you never told me, Miss MacNeil," he murmured, bringing his face closer to hers, "just what kind of fool put a diamond like that on your finger and then let you run off—with a sixteen-year-old boy—to live at a strange man's house. In Nashville. Of all places."

Dinah knew she should try to resist but found herself incapable, as if his touch had enchanted her, robbing her of will or reason. "Let go," she said weakly. She looked into his eyes and found them more mesmerizing, more mocking than ever. "Why—" she breathed unevenly "—why do you say Nashville 'of all places'?"

He drew her more firmly into his arms. "Because," he muttered, lowering his lips until they almost brushed hers, "one of the things Nashville is about is passion."

She felt his hands move with suspenseful slowness until one found the small of her back and pulled her more intimately against him. The other rose to her nape and began to caress the golden silk of her hair. Her senses careened. Her very blood seemed aroused by something wonderful and fearful.

"Passion," he repeated softly. His lips parted. So did hers. His mouth moved the barest fraction of an inch nearer, so that their faces almost touched.

The he let his lips rest on hers lightly, in the most teasing of kisses. Shocked by her acquiescence, Dinah went cold and stony in his arms. But she could not will the feeling from her lips. His mouth taunted hers, daring her to respond. Instinctively she closed her eyes and was dizzied by the combination of the darkness, his nearness and the seductive heat of his lips.

She wanted him to kiss her, yet the thought terrified her. Then, as if impatient with her indecision and shyness, he pulled her more tightly toward him, so she had to gasp involuntarily for breath. His lips took hers fully then, with a dominant completeness that dazzled her. The tormenting fervor of his kiss breathed a swiftly growing desire in her, sweeping through her like wildfire.

Again she gave a little gasp, half of fright, half of newly awakened yearning. The tip of his tongue brushed warmly against the fullness of her mouth, then delved within to take even fuller possession of her. Truly frightened now, Dinah still could not resist him. She felt her breasts tingle with excitement as his body crushed hers to him. Foreign urges swept through her, filling her with heat at the same time the ice of fear made her incapable of moving.

Then he drew back, letting his hands leave her body slowly. He reached out and straightened the high collar of her dress, a glint of satisfaction in his eyes.

"See?" he said flippantly. "You're learning. You need to keep learning. You're just a child, Miss MacNeil. For all your brittle words, you kiss like a girl who's been taught never to show her feelings—or even admit them. What a pity. The good folk of Kakexia have sent me a child to guard another child. Although as children go, you're an extremely uppity one. Don't worry. I'll humble you. And educate you."

He delivered this speech with infinite self-satisfaction, his hands still toying provocatively with her collar. "Don't let the kiss bother you," he murmured. "Forget it. It really wasn't worth remembering."

His hands dropped away, and he turned and strolled toward the stairs. She was taken aback by his arrogance and by her own stupidity. "I should have slapped your face," she called out angrily. She put more emotion in the words then she had into the embrace.

He didn't pause, but he tossed her a solemn look over his shoulder. "Definitely," he replied, mouth drawn down soberly. "You should have." Then his white grin flashed in all its glory. "But you didn't. Maybe there's hope for you."

He descended the stairs, whistling softly to himself. Dinah marched into her room, refraining from slamming the door. But she hurled horrid little pillows shaped like hearts all over the floor, and then flung herself on the red satin coverlet and beat it with her fists.

Who was this man? she demanded of herself. What sort of sorcery had he worked on her? She had been with Dennis all these years and not once had he made her feel this way. And Dennis was good, kind, trustworthy, faithful, honest and dependable—perfect in fact. What was happening to her?

She had no answer. She looked around her room in dismay. There were hearts all over the floor. And on the wall, numberless satyrs expertly pursued nymphs who all seemed, to their bewilderment, to be losing ground.

CHAPTER FOUR

"CAN'T YOU TAKE OFF that hat once in a while?" Dinah asked plaintively. She was nervous and filled with self-doubt. Both emotions were foreign to her.

"No," Roscoe answered, truly shocked. "This is my lucky hat."

"Umm," Dinah replied in defeat. After the previous night, she felt too apprehensive to argue. She and Roscoe had risen early and were taking breakfast on the patio. Roscoe, recovered from his trip, was wide-eyed at the mansion's excesses, and his appetite had returned with a vengeance. He had never tasted a croissant before and ate seven, as well as half a pound of bacon and six fried eggs.

Dinah, on the other hand, had no appetite at all. She was too disturbed by her encounter with Mitch Carey. She dreaded seeing him, and she wished she hadn't committed herself to trying to find Roscoe a better offer. She realized that nothing in her very fine education had prepared her for such a challenge, or for dealing with a man like Mitch.

To her discomfort, Mitch appeared just as Roscoe was finishing his last croissant. Lithe, his dark hair shining blue-black in the sun, he came strolling through the azalea beds. He wore white jeans that fit him as smoothly and snugly as skin fits a snake. Sockless, he was shod in Italian sandals, and his hand-knit cotton sweater matched the sea-foam green of his eyes.

Dinah reached for her coffee cup feigning disinterest. To her humiliation, her hand shook so perceptibly that she had to set the cup down. Self-consciously she clasped her hands and hid them in the lap of her full paisley skirt. Her heart beat so swiftly that she imagined Mitch could see it pounding beneath her white ruffled shirt.

But he hardly noticed her. His white smile was wide, friendly and directed at Roscoe. He put the boy at ease as if by magic. That accomplished, he finally deigned to look at Dinah. His smile was still wide, and friendly, but the very spirit of the devil played in his eyes.

"Miss MacNeil," he said in his mocking drawl. "How fresh you look—like a flower just opening to the sun. I almost feel as if I should bow to you—as to a true Victorian lady."

"Thank you," she replied civilly. She wished she had the coffee cup so she could fling it at his head. In a few words he had scoffed at not only her character, but at her wardrobe, as well. Just because her tastes were traditional, Mitch Carey had no right to speak to her as if she were a hopeless prig.

He turned his attention to Roscoe. "I imagine Miss MacNeil will be taking you around Nashville today to talk to people. I'd like her to bring you by my studio at about four. All right?"

"Sure," agreed Roscoe, but he looked vaguely troubled. "What people?"

Dinah opened her mouth to explain she simply wanted to interview a few people before Roscoe made a commitment to Diamond Horseshoe. Mitch cut her off before she could speak.

"Miss MacNeil is here to watch out for you," he told the boy smoothly. "She wants to make sure she can trust me.

She imagines she can get a better offer for you. Don't worry.
My offer's best. She'll see.''

Roscoe looked at Mitch, then at Dinah, then back at
Mitch. "I—I thought everything was settled." He could not
disguise a nervous gulp.

Again Dinah started to offer a tactfully vague explanation. But Mitch was too quick. "You know how women
are," he said, smiling and putting his hand on Roscoe's
shoulder in a brotherly gesture. "They're never happy unless you let them shop around. We're going to have to let her
shop. Get it out of her system. She'll come around if we're
patient.''

"But—'' Roscoe said and gulped again.

Of all the male chauvinist ways to explain it, Dinah
thought hotly. Her blouse might be Victorian, but the breast
beneath it burned with a savage fire.

"Don't worry,'' Mitch assured Roscoe. "Miss MacNeil's
intelligent. She'll soon see our arrangement is the best. I
think you can trust her, son. I'm almost sure you can. And
in the meantime, while she's learning her lesson, you'll get
to see a little of Nashville.''

Flashing another smile, Mitch said he had to get to his
office, then left.

She stared after him in smoldering disbelief. How dared
he assure Roscoe that she was trustworthy? It was like the
wolf telling the lamb that the shepherdess might be all right.

Roscoe was staring uneasily at her from under the brim of
his hat. "You don't like him," the boy said quietly. "How
come? I do. I thought he'd be old and scary. But he ain't.''

"You can't tell if you should trust somebody just by
talking to them for ten minutes," she answered. Now that
Mitch was gone, her hands no longer trembled. She picked
up her cup and finished her coffee as if it would give her
needed strength.

"Well," Roscoe said with a shrug. "I reckon you go by feelins on this sort of thing. On any sort of thing."

"Feelings," Dinah replied darkly. She wished she had no feelings. She wished she were back in Connecticut. She wished she were walking down the aisle to marry Dennis at this very moment.

"If you can't trust your feelins, what can you trust?" Roscoe asked simply.

Dinah couldn't reply to that. "We need to go see some people," she said at last. "For your sake."

"You're doin' it again," Roscoe observed. He reached for her unfinished croissant and popped it into his mouth.

Dinah was too rattled to correct his manners. "I'm doing what?"

"You're twistin' on that ring of yours like you're tryin' to unscrew your finger."

With a start she looked down. She had been twisting Dennis's ring around as if she was determined to remove it.

It was her turn to swallow nervously. "We need to go see some people in the city," she repeated.

HER DAY proved to be a long and grueling exercise in humility. The name MacNeil had opened several doors for her, but others stayed tightly shut. No recording company, no producer, hardly anyone connected with the music business would talk to her. Only one agent, Stephen Fleetwood, would see her but not until later in the week. Ironically, he was the man Mitch had recommended most highly. She didn't know whether to trust Stephen Fleetwood but had no other choice.

Everywhere else she called, answers were polite but firm. Nobody wanted to give her or Roscoe the time of day. There were thousands of people begging for entrance into the kingdom of music. She and Roscoe were just another part of the faceless horde. Dinah felt with sinking certainty that Mitch Carey's offer was not only going to be Roscoe's best chance, it would be his only chance. She was trapped. She had to contend with the man.

The only people who agreed to see her that day were the lawyers her father had recommended. Their opinions should have cheered her but did not.

Mitch's offer was not only fair, but it was extraordinarily generous, said the first attorney she consulted. Roscoe was a very lucky boy, continued the solemn Mr. Roman Hornsby, who looked like an owl. "No," said Mr. Hornsby, he knew nothing of Carey personally except that he already had a reputation for being smart, aggressive and confident. "Yes," said Mr. Hornsby, the names of agents and so forth Mitch had suggested for Roscoe were the names of some of the fastest rising young business talents in Nashville. And that certainly included the formidable agent Stephen Fleetwood.

The second lawyer, the young and animated Richard Ortison, gave Dinah precisely the same information. He looked over Mitch's offer and whistled softly. "Are you a religious woman?" he asked, gray eyes twinkling.

"Why?" she responded in surprise.

"Because—" he grinned, cocking his curly red head "—if you are, you should get down on your knees and thank heaven for an offer like this. There are a thousand people in Nashville who'd sell their souls for a chance like this. Don't just accept this offer, Miss MacNeil—grab it and cherish it. Your young friend Mr. Hockenberry is extraordinarily fortunate. Extraordinarily."

When they left Ortison's book-lined office, Dinah was depressed and Roscoe was elated.

"See?" he said, pushing his hat up so he could see her more clearly. "I told you Mr. Carey was all right. You just got to trust your feelins."

"Roscoe," she replied patiently, "your feelings said to trust him, and my feelings said not to trust him. So your theory has a flaw and we had to check the man out."

Roscoe pondered for a moment. He frowned. He shook his head. "Nope. I think you're confusin' your business feelins with your woman feelins and it has discombobulated you."

"What?" she demanded, horrified. "What's that supposed to mean?" Where did the boy get such ideas?

Roscoe blushed and apologized, but his words kept echoing in her mind. He was correct. She was discombobulated. Thoroughly and completely. She doubted that a more discombobulated woman existed. So she and Roscoe had continued to drift for the rest of the day from closed door to closed door, from one refusal to another.

DINAH SAT, footsore and humbled, in Bootsie's Barbecue Parlor, staring at the autographed photographs of singers and musicians. Roscoe was happily eating a hamburger and drinking a large glass of milk. Since his appetite had returned, he was as hard to fill up as the legendary bottomless pit.

She should have eaten something but couldn't. She drank black coffee, although it simply added to her nervousness. Both her nerves and her stomach demanded more sustenance, but she couldn't bear the thought of food. She sat brooding on her failures. How naive she had been to think she could simply walk into Nashville and find Roscoe a better offer than Mitch Carey's. Thoughts of the man seemed to have taken control of her mind. Why hadn't she gone straight back to Connecticut?

"I think I could eat another one of these here hamburgers," Roscoe offered, bringing Dinah back to herself. She looked at him with a start. Yes, it was true, she really was sitting in a barbecue restaurant in the middle of Nashville, and she really was responsible for this genial scarecrow of a boy. And she was going to have to tell Mitch Carey that he'd been right and she'd been wrong. It hadn't taken her a week to learn it. It had taken her less than a day.

She sighed and glanced at her watch. "It's close to four," she said. "We need to meet Mr. Carey. And you need to save some room for supper."

Tired and confused, she paid their bill. She didn't want to see Mitch. Something about the mere thought made her hands tremble.

What's wrong with me? she wondered in agitation. No man she'd ever met had ever affected her so. *Discombobulated*, she thought, remembering Roscoe's words. Her business and woman feelings were mixed up—badly. She wished she were home with safe, sweet, dependable Dennis. He had never upset her woman feelings one whit.

THE SHABBY NARROW BRICK BUILDING that housed Diamond Horseshoe Records wasn't impressive, but the amount of activity taking place inside it was. The company's fortunes were obviously on the rise, for workmen swarmed everywhere. No music stirred the air, only the cacophony of pounding, drilling, sawing and the thud-thud-thud of a gigantic cement mixer. Mitch was renovating. In a big way.

His secretary sat stoically at her desk, wearing a shower cap to keep the floating plaster dust out of her hair. She was a large, sensible-looking fiftyish woman, not at all the sort Dinah had imagined.

"I'm Mrs. Buttress! Please excuse the temporary disorder!" she yelled. Somehow the woman was able to yell with both calm and dignity. "The present confusion will result in a future order and efficiency that will enable Diamond Horseshoe to carry out its purpose with maximum effectiveness. Mr. Carey will see you in his office." She rose, adjusted her shower cap briskly and opened the office door for Dinah and Roscoe. The woman moved with such disciplined precision that Dinah half expected her to execute a military salute before she withdrew from the room.

The building might be in chaos, but Mitch was cool and in perfect control. His office, she thanked the Fates, was soundproof, an island of quiet in the madness of remodeling.

He sat at a huge battered desk. He still wore his tight white jeans and the pale green sweater that matched his eyes. His feet in their Italian sandals were crossed casually on his desk top. The sharp angle of his widow's peak, the knavish arch of his brows made him look like a man who could have been an eminently successful highwayman in a previous century. She could almost imagine him in riding breeches, a flowing shirt, a brace of pistols on his lean hips.

He shook Roscoe's hand, greeting him amiably. He ignored Dinah. "Roscoe," Mitch practically purred, "you've met Lucky Bucky Williston before. He's my promotions man—for the time being."

"Pleasedtameetcha, sonny," Lucky Bucky grunted, struggling to rise. He pumped Roscoe's hand with an excess of zeal. "Gonna be working a lot with you. Redesignin' your image."

"My which?" Roscoe asked uncertainly.

"Just leave it to me, son," Lucky Bucky advised. "I got ideas for you. I got a million of 'em."

Mitch finally noticed Dinah. "Bucky, have you met Miss MacNeil? She's Roscoe's guardian for this trip. Miss MacNeil, Lucky Bucky Williston."

"Charmed, you bet your butter beans," Lucky Bucky said with an unctuous grin. He swept off his orange Stetson and bowed. Dinah fought a wave of revulsion. The man was huge, obese almost. He bulged in a burnt-orange cowboy suit with black sequined steers' heads ornamenting the lapels.

"You're a cute little heifer," Bucky said, beaming and giving her a leer that made her blush with both anger and embarrassment. "Mitch said you was a little bit of a thing in ruffles and high necklines that kept you all covered up. You do look the perfect schoolteacher, ma'am, and that's a fact, though purtier than most. Maybe purtier than all." He grinned widely at her, as if he thought the grin was dazzling and seductive. Then he winked.

Dinah was certain she heard his fat eyelid go snap when he closed it. Dressed in orange, he looked like a gigantic lecherous pumpkin. Her face was stiff with distaste. "Thank you," she said icily. Lucky Bucky didn't seem to notice the frost in her words. Mitch did, and he didn't try to hide his smile.

"And how has the rest of your day been, Miss Mac-Neil?" Mitch asked mockingly. "I hope you don't have an exclusive five-year contract for Roscoe with RCA or Columbia. I hope the *federales* aren't coming after me because of unsavory business secrets you've unearthed."

Dinah's day had been dispiriting and mortifying. She would not tell Mitch, however. His audaciously cool eyes made her mind and body feel as chaotic as the scene beyond the door, where everything was in turmoil.

"My day was perfectly fine," she said in an even voice. He flashed his grin. He knew she was lying.

"Sit," he said, waving her and Roscoe toward a rather ratty pair of armchairs. Roscoe sat dutifully. His hat slid over his eyes and he pushed it back up. Dinah sat down as primly as a Puritan maiden.

Mitch picked up a pencil, tossed it so it spun in the air, then caught it expertly. "We have some major decisions to discuss," he said. "Things that—if we decide to work together—will affect Roscoe's entire career."

Roscoe shifted in his chair, looking both nervous and excited. Lucky Bucky had sunk into another spindly armchair that looked as if it would collapse beneath his weight. Mitch tossed his pencil and caught it again.

"Wait a minute," Dinah said, caught off guard. "Before you start talking about decisions that will affect his whole career—his whole life—shouldn't somebody experienced be here to represent his interests?"

"Did you hire anyone to do that?" Mitch asked, smiling sardonically.

"No," Dinah replied, taken aback. "Of course not."

"I gave you a whole list of agents to consult. Did you get in touch with any of them?"

She nodded numbly. "But I haven't had time to see anyone yet," she began. He had to know that.

"Then," he mused with an elaborate shrug, "I guess you'll have to represent him for now. There's no one else here to do it, is there?"

That's right, she thought grimly. *There's no one else to do it for the boy. Just me. One inexperienced woman—who's been off balance since she met you.*

He took her silence for assent. "I'm glad you're finally being sensible and cooperative," he said in a low voice. "First, out of deference to our little...agreement, Miss MacNeil, I won't ask Roscoe to start rehearsing until next week."

Her heart sank and beat harder and more unevenly. Their "little agreement" had done nothing except allow her to make a fool of herself. But she could not admit that in front of Roscoe and Lucky Bucky.

"Normally," he continued silkily, "we'd do the rehearsing here. I'm having the facilities overhauled and expanded, however, so that's impossible. I'll rent a place to rehearse. And to record. I want state-of-the-art equipment."

Roscoe looked delighted. Dinah merely nodded mechanically.

"I've gone to the liberty of picking out the studio musicians to play with Roscoe," he went on. "They'll rehearse for a week. If he has trouble with any of them, it's your duty to inform me so we can clear it up. Understand?"

"I understand," she replied aloofly. His condescending tone implied he thought he was talking to a simpleton. He probably talked to all women that way.

"And now," Mitch said, his smile disappearing, "Bucky says he has some ideas for us to consider."

"Ideas are my middle name," Bucky said, narrowing his eyes in self-admiration. "I have ideas the way a dog has fleas. Now listen to this. Nashville's been accused of gettin' too slick. People are saying it needs to go back to its country roots. Look at Roscoe. There he sits, country as a cowpie. My idea is this. Let's present him to the public as a real old-fashioned country boy. Dress him in patched overalls. Have hay stickin' out of his hat. And here's the gimmick—whenever he goes on stage, he's got a live pig with him. We'll say it's his treasured pet. What do you think?"

Lucky Bucky leaned back in his chair, looking proud and smug. Roscoe's expression was one of dazed sickness. Mitch's face was bored and unreadable. He flipped his pencil again. Dinah sat on the edge of her seat, appalled.

"No," she said firmly.

Bucky sat back in displeased surprise. "What do you mean, no? Why not?"

"No," she replied quietly, clenching her hands, "because that is the worst, most demeaning, most ludicrous, tasteless idea I've ever heard. *A pig!* No! Absolutely not!"

"Okay," Lucky Bucky said. "We'll drop the pig. But we keep the idea of the kid as a comical country hayseed."

Dinah straightened in her chair regally. She could feel the blood pounding in her temples, but somehow she kept her voice calm. "Mr. Williston, I said no. Emphatically. You will not make him into an object of laughter. He's a singer, not a clown. Drop the whole idea. Please!"

"Fine, fine, fine," he said, raising pudgy hands as if to defend himself. "But it's a natural. I mean he's got that tooth out. He's skinny. He's got that weird squint to his eyes."

Roscoe sank more deeply into his chair, looking stricken. Mitch's eyes were trained on Dinah now, with an intensity that belied his lazy expression. His unwavering gaze increased her agitation, but she struggled to stay firm and centered.

"I'm going to make appointments to get his tooth fixed and his eyes tested," Dinah stated with cold passion. "And there's no need to belittle him. He'll dress decently or he won't get on stage for you at all."

"You don't understand. You really should think about this—" Lucky Bucky started to object. Mitch, his eyes still on Dinah, interrupted him.

"The lady doesn't like the idea, Bucky. And as you can see, she's a stubborn little thing. Try something else. After all, our friend Roscoe here looks as good as any of us did at sixteen. When he fills out, he'll be a handsome enough fellow."

Dinah blinked in surprise. Mitch had jeered at her as usual. But what he said about Roscoe was true. How odd she had never noticed that the boy just might turn into a handsome young man one day.

Lucky Bucky was eyeing the boy, too, as if he were a prey that had to be properly stalked. "All right, all right," he muttered. "Fix the tooth, fix his eyes, get twenty pounds on him—you're right. Not a bad-looking kid. So who says basic country can't go with good-lookin'? Fatten him up, get him a couple of rhinestone suits, pay girls in the audience to faint when he sings. Change his name. How about Ross Hocken? How about Ray 'Heartbreaker' Hockes? If he's not going to be a clodhopper, he should drop the clodhopper name."

Mitch said nothing. He arched one brow at Dinah. The corner of his mouth went up. She knew what he meant—it was her move. She glanced at Roscoe. He looked pale, but a muscle jumped in his jaw. She knew that he was affronted, and deeply.

"Roscoe?" she said quietly. "I know what I think. What do you think?"

The muscles jumped again. "Roscoe Hockenberry is my name and it was my daddy's name before me," he said to Lucky Bucky. "It's a name I'm proud of. I ain't changin' it."

Mitch smiled at her more openly, as if in challenge. She tried to ignore what his white smile and teasing green eyes were doing to her pulse.

"I agree," she said crisply. "Roscoe is not a comedian. He is not a sex idol. He's a singer. He doesn't need rhinestone suits. Or fainting girls. Nor, I'm afraid, does he need you, Mr. Williston, if you won't treat him with more dignity."

Dinah's boldness astonished her. She felt absolutely giddy. The ruffles on her breast rose and fell swiftly, and Mitch studied their movement with indolent interest.

Lucky Bucky glared at her, mortally offended. "I'm the one that knows this business, little lady. I'm the expert. You deal with Diamond Horseshoe and you deal with me."

Mitch kept watching her ruffles. He pretended to stifle a yawn. If he was waiting to see if she could really fend for Roscoe, she would show him.

"You deal with Roscoe Hockenberry, and you deal with me," she said levelly to Bucky. "Roscoe came here to sing, not to be a circus act. He's serious about his job. I wish I could say the same about you. I'm appalled by your attitude."

Lucky Bucky swelled with anger. His face turned a deep red that clashed with his orange suit and hat. "Nobody," he thundered, "has ever had the audacity to tell me I'm not serious about my job. Especially no uppity little Yankee girl who don't know diddly-squat about the music business."

Now I've done it, Dinah thought, caught between anger and terror. Roscoe's eyes widened in apprehension, as if he could see his career crumbling into rubble before it even began.

Mitch stirred in his chair, his mouth twisting wryly. "Wrong, Bucky," Mitch drawled. "Somebody has had the audacity to tell you just that. And it happens to be this uppity little Yankee here. What's more, she's the one we have to deal with. Find another approach."

Saved, Dinah thought with a flood of relief. Lucky Bucky grew paler and Roscoe visibly relaxed. She suddenly felt almost faint. She had eaten hardly anything all day. She was trying to fight men far more powerful and knowledgeable than she, and she had no weapon other than raw courage. Why had she challenged Lucky Bucky so openly? Yet what else could she have done? Her head ached. She felt hollow and shaky.

Mitch studied her pallid face. "I think we've established some of our central feelings. We've talked enough for one day. We all know where we stand. We'll continue this tomorrow. In the meantime, Bucky, rethink the way to present Roscoe. It's your job to be flexible."

"Yessir," said Lucky Bucky sullenly. He gave Dinah a hostile look. Oddly, it only made made her feel more light-headed.

Lucky Bucky rose, massive and cold as an iceberg. "I'm flexible as a snake," he asserted. "The question is, how will this woman know a good idea when she hears one?"

"We'll just have to hope, won't we, Bucky?" Mitch smiled.

Dinah went a little paler with suppressed anger. Bucky said his goodbyes without grace and stamped from the office. Mitch turned his attention to Roscoe.

"Don't worry about this," he assured the boy. "We're going ahead as if nothing's happened. I'm bringing Mrs. Buttress home with us tonight. I want her to transcribe the songs you've written that you think are best. You and she can work on that after supper."

"Yessir," Roscoe replied. In relief, he gave his lopsided grin.

Dinah stood, still feeling slightly shaky. Roscoe, following her lead, rose, too. He smiled at her as if he were proud of her.

She'd have to see about getting that boy's tooth fixed, she thought dreamily. She'd have to make an appointment to have his eyes examined, his hair cut. She needed to buy him new jeans. And she had to call Vesta that night. And she should talk to Willard.... She should have stopped at the library to get some books on the music business ...

Dinah would have been all right had she made it outside to the fresh air. She would have been fine. But just as she and Roscoe were poised to leave, Dinah saw something dark stalk from behind a bookcase and cross the carpet. Her heart stopped. An enormous black mouse marched over the floor, straight toward her. It was certainly the most enormous and malicious-looking mouse in the universe. She felt the universe quake slightly, acknowledging the fact.

"Miss MacNeil," Mitch was saying. "Miss MacNeil. Are you all right?"

"I'm fine," she answered, but her voice sounded far away and wispy. When had she sat back down? she wondered. When had Mitch sprung to his feet?

Roscoe had his hat off and was chasing the creature, which ducked behind a filing cabinet and disappeared. "Woo, you old mouse! Git!" yelled Roscoe. He stamped his foot and turned. "He's gone, ma'am," he said, jamming his hat back on his head. "It's all right."

Mitch looked at her in disbelief. Slowly a smile lit his tanned face. Dinah couldn't stand the derision in his eyes. She stood up quickly. Too quickly. The next thing she knew she was in Mitch's arms. Her knees refused to support her.

She gazed up dazedly into dark-lashed green eyes that were suddenly serious. His brows drew together in a concerned frown. His mouth was grim, and for the first time she noticed what strong, chiseled lips he had. She fought to retain consciousness. She concentrated on his eyes, the strength and fire in them. He looked at her so intently that it was as if he willed her to come back to herself.

Instinctively she put her hand on his chest, resting it against the pale green of his sweater. He covered her small hand with his warm bronzed one, pressing it more firmly against him. She could feel the powerful beating of his heart.

"Your fingers are like ice," he said softly. He took his hand from hers and skimmed his fingertips over the smoothness of her cheek. "And you're as pale as the underside of a flower petal." He smoothed her silky blond hair back from her forehead. Then he touched her cheek again. "What's wrong with you?" he demanded. His voice was low but harsh. "Don't tell me you're actually afraid of mice?"

"I—I—" Dinah began. She struggled briefly to stand on her own, but his arms were both forceful and comforting. Gratefully she let herself rest in his superior strength. "I guess I haven't eaten today, at least not much, and everything's so strange—so tense—" She felt too shaken to try to lie. "Yes. I'm terrified of mice."

"Damn! It's unbelievable." The green eyes glinted fire and amusement. "Roscoe," he ordered, never taking his gaze from Dinah, "go across the street to that little restaurant and bring back some orange juice. If you need money get it from Mrs. Buttress."

"Yessir!" She heard Roscoe's scurrying footsteps. As the door slammed, she felt herself being swept up into Mitch's arms as if she were light as a doll.

"Good Lord," he muttered. "You don't weigh more than a feather. What are you—ninety-five pounds?"

"Ninety," Dinah said weakly. Without thinking she had locked her hands behind his neck. Once again she felt she was drawing strength from his sinewy warmth. But his movement made her dizzier, so she had to close her eyes again. She heard a door being kicked open. She felt herself being lowered to something that felt mercifully soft and safe, yet she didn't trust herself to take her hands from the powerful column of Mitch's neck.

"Where are we?" she asked in confusion, her lids fluttering open. The sight of his green eyes and the arrogant arch of his brows stimulated her yet made her feel even fainter.

"Inner office," he said without smiling. "Rank doth have its privileges. You're resting on what was once somebody's casting couch."

"Mr. Carey?" The capable tone of Mrs. Buttress rang from the door of the outer office. "Mr. Hockenberry said Miss MacNeil had fainted. Should I call a medical person?"

Mrs. Buttress's no-nonsense voice brought Dinah back to reality. She released her hold on Mitch, her hands flying away as if in guilt. She tried to sink more deeply into the couch to put more distance between her face and his sternly handsome one.

"I think she'll live, Mrs. Buttress," Mitch said ironically. "Just close the door. It's noisy as blazes out there."

Mrs. Buttress obeyed and the chaotic noise of the workmen ceased.

"Alone at last," he said. He smiled at her obvious discomfort as she squirmed in embarrassment. He touched her throat beside her jaw. "Pulse is better. Speeding up quite nicely. We're getting a very healthy pulse indeed there."

Dinah would have wriggled away in shame, but he had her pinned neatly against the back of the couch. "Let me alone," she protested. "I'm fine—really."

He just smiled again. "Really, MacNeil, you're a disappointment. This is disgusting."

"What do you mean?" She couldn't take her eyes from the provocative curve of his lips.

"I thought you were going to have the strength to be an opponent, a worthy adversary. Look at you. You dissolved after the first really good encounter. You're no fun. You fall right over."

She stared up at him, her emotions tumultuous. She wanted to hit him. She also wanted to be kissed by him. The realization astounded her. "I didn't actually faint," she returned. "I did not fall over."

"You would have—" he shrugged "—if I hadn't caught you. Are you saying this isn't weakness on your part? Then what is it—wiles? You wanted to be in my arms again? Should I be flattered, or frightened? I've never had an heiress try to charm me. You swoon very well. Do they teach that at the best schools?"

She could only lie there, staring up indignantly at his taunting expression. She knew he was teasing her, but she couldn't help defending herself. "I'm not weak," she said between her teeth. "I don't use wiles. I simply have a phobia about mice. It's embarrassing, but it's true. I had a bad day and I've hardly eaten, and then this huge rodent charged me— Oh, stop smiling that way! Will you let me up?"

She struggled to sit up and he let her. She paid for her determination with another wave of dizziness. "Oh!" she gasped.

He swore and made her lower her head to increase the flow of blood to her brain. "Put your head between your knees," he ordered.

"No!" she cried, but his hand was clasping the back of her neck and forcing her to do as he said.

"What's wrong with you?" he demanded. "If you don't want to faint, keep your head between your knees, dammit."

"I refuse," Dinah protested. "I refuse to let you see me looking so ridiculous. You'll just laugh harder."

"Women!" he said with such withering scorn that she was grateful that her face was hidden in the voluminous folds of her skirt. "Why couldn't they have sent the football coach with Roscoe? Some good old boy I could have talked with man-to-man? Instead, I had to get you. You'll back down Lucky Bucky, a man three times your size, then go woozy when you see a scared little mouse. What am I supposed to make of you?''

She heard the outer door of the office open. ''Anybody here?'' came Roscoe's tentative voice.

''We're back here,'' Mitch called, his impatience with Dinah still edging his tone. Putting his arm around her, he allowed her to sit up again. She was still dizzy, whether from the day's events or Mitch's nearness she wasn't sure.

''Is she all right?'' asked Roscoe, looking nervous.

''I'm perfectly fine,'' Dinah said, but her voice was shaky. She tried to move away from Mitch's protecting embrace, but he held her fast. Her heart pounded so wildly that surely he could feel it beating against his chest.

''She's not perfectly fine,'' Mitch said in disgust. ''Listen, you've got to watch her from now on. See that she eats. She's too... too little. She can't go without food.''

''She didn't eat much today,'' Roscoe admitted helplessly. ''That's for certain sure. And she ain't never liked mice, that's a fact. But I ain't sure but that she's got another problem.''

There was a beat of silence. *Another problem,* thought Dinah in confusion. What did he mean? Roscoe was creative, but creativity filled him with peculiar ideas.

''Another problem?'' Mitch asked suspiciously. He held her more tightly. ''With her health? What do you mean?''

''I think her ring's too tight,'' Roscoe said earnestly.

There was another silence. Dinah's face burned. She would have gladly shot Roscoe, except he looked so perfectly innocent.

Then Mitch's laughter broke loose. ''Roscoe, my boy!'' he exclaimed in wonder. ''You're a poet—and a philosopher, too. You're right. I think her ring is too tight. Way too tight. Here, Dinah, drink your juice. The fire within you wants fuel.''

She didn't want the juice, but Mitch forced her to drink it. "Roscoe," he instructed, "go tell Mrs. Buttress to call the exterminators and get them in here tonight. All this construction work has stirred up the local mice. We'll have to make sure they evacuate before Miss MacNeil returns."

Roscoe obeyed.

Mitch took the empty juice glass from Dinah's hand and set it on a nearby table. He kept his arm firmly around her. It seemed to burn into her slender shoulders, filling her chest with disturbing warmth.

"I'm fine," she muttered nervously. "Move your arm, please."

He didn't move it. He leaned closer, his voice insinuating. "A wise old man once told me," he breathed, "to find an old-fashioned girl. He actually said to me, 'Son, if you find a girl who can still faint at the sight of a mouse, marry her.' Now I've found you—" he took her hand and turned it so her diamond flashed "—and you're taken. Already reserved. What do we do now?''

She drew her hand away, pulled from his embrace and stood. She forced herself to stand firmly, with no sign of weakness or wavering. She refused to look at him, because he so troubled the core of her wildly beating heart.

"We don't do anything," she said.

"We'll see about that," he drawled. Then he smiled.

CHAPTER FIVE

DINAH SAT ALONE in her room, running her hand meditatively over the red satin spread. Her window was open. The white drapes stirred in the breeze, and Roscoe's voice came drifting up from the patio. He was singing an eerily haunting love song.

Between songs, the breeze had borne to her incomprehensible scraps of conversation, the voices of Roscoe, Mrs. Buttress and Mitch. Dinah had elected to have supper alone in her room. Now she felt unaccountably lonely, and the words of Roscoe's song kept echoing in her mind:

I didn't want to love you, Fallen Angel.
Now I've fallen, too.
How hard I've fallen—
What will I do?
What will I do?
What will I do?

She rose and shut the window. She locked it, as if she could lock out the thoughts that tormented her. She tried not to think of the maddening dark-haired man who was responsible for her being in Nashville. She didn't want to recall her own stupid weakness and that she had almost fainted in his office. She didn't want to think at all.

Irritably, she wondered why Roscoe's songs should bother her. What could the boy know about love, anyway? Nothing, she told herself, except what he'd learned from other songs and from fairy tales about love. She had always been too wise, too mature to believe such fictions.

She sat on the heart-shaped bed again. She wore what her brother called one of her "sissy dresses." A white knee-length smock with long puffed sleeves and a high ruffled neck, it was the sort of dress she'd always loved—quaint and winsome. Now it simply made her think of how Mitch liked to goad her about being "Victorian."

She wished she had something to do. All her life when loneliness threatened, she had opened a book and found refuge. But for the first time, she couldn't concentrate. Her book, a new biography of Mary Queen of Scots, lay unopened on the bedside table.

She had made the phone calls she had to make. Before supper, she and Roscoe had called Vesta and then Willard. Roscoe had looked seriously homesick for the first time, and Dinah had promised Vesta repeatedly that she would look after the woman's only remaining son. She assured Willard, none too truthfully, that she felt perfectly confident. But the demands of the situation had exhausted her and she had been glad to flee to the privacy of her room. Now it seemed like a large and gaudy cell.

She wished she were outside in the cool evening where the whippoorwills sang. But if she were, she would be sitting by Mitch, feeling his nearness....

Don't be ridiculous, she told herself, her mind veering in the opposite direction. If she felt attracted to Mitch Carey it was because he appealed to some small, uncivilized part of her that she hadn't known existed. Now that she knew, she would simply subdue and ignore it.

Besides, the man was her opponent, she reminded herself. He was testing her, trying her, pushing her, for no other reason than it gave him perverse pleasure. If he wasn't actually her enemy, he employed a man who was, at least after this afternoon. Lucky Bucky Williston had practically forced her to oppose his ideas, and she had been bred to stand up for her principles.

The less she saw of both men the better, she thought starkly. She must keep her emotional distance so that she could handle them—for Roscoe's sake and her own. She was, after all, Roscoe's guardian and Dennis's fiancée—not the kind of woman who took promises lightly.

Her emotions vaulted off in a new direction and suddenly she missed Dennis. Why had she ever doubted, even secretly, that she and Dennis were meant for each other? They had practically been raised together. They were two of a kind: bookish, quiet, undemonstrative and proud of it.

Although she and Dennis had talked on the phone briefly the day before, she needed to hear his reassuring, cheery voice again. She lifted the receiver of the jeweled phone and dialed his number. Their conversation the previous day had been short and strangely impersonal. Dinah had been too tired from the trip to wish it otherwise. Now she needed Dennis and needed him badly.

Instead of Dennis she reached an answering machine with a recording of his burbling voice. "Hello! Hello! This is Dennis Lingle. The symphony is having an extra practice tonight, so like the little angel I am, I'll be playing the harp. At the sound of the beep, please leave your name and number, and I'll call you sometime tomorrow. Ta-ta!"

Dinah's fingers tightened on the rhinestone-encrusted receiver. She heard the beep. "Dennis," she said desperately. "This is Di. Nashville is more complicated than I could have imagined. I may have bitten off more than I can chew. I need to talk to someone. Could you call me? I—I miss you."

She hung up, feeling shaky and empty again, as when she'd almost fainted. Dennis wouldn't call tonight. Dennis never called after ten o'clock on a weeknight. He would not even listen to his answering machine tape because it might contain disturbing news that would interfere with his sleep. Dennis, so generous in most matters, was very particular about his bedtime. "If Dennis doesn't get his proper sleep," his mother would say fondly, "he just isn't Mr. Sunshine anymore. There's a little bit of Mr. Grumpity-Grump in him."

Sitting on the bed, Dinah unconsciously twisted the large diamond on her finger. Then, realizing what she was doing, she made a sound of exasperation. She reached for the phone again and did something she had seldom done since starting college—she called home, just to talk.

MacNeil children were raised to be disciplined. Dinah, as the youngest of the clan, considered herself the most disciplined of all. Her youth, her smallness, her childhood illnesses had all made her try doubly hard to fulfill the MacNeil ideals of orderliness and self-control.

But she suddenly felt young and unsure of herself. She needed her mother's assurance of how perfectly she and Dennis were matched. But her parents didn't answer. They weren't at home. She talked to Svetla, the cook, who said that the judge was at a convention in Boston, and that Mrs. MacNeil was spending the weekend at Bar Harbor with Muffy, Dennis's mother.

"No," Dinah said, fighting dejection, she didn't wish to leave a message. She hung up the phone and stared at it. Its false jewels glittered and seemed to stare back.

A soft knock at the door startled her out of her melancholy. She leaped up, not bothering to put on her shoes. She swung the door open slowly.

It was Mitch. Casual as ever, he had changed into black linen slacks and an olive-green silk shirt rolled up to show his tanned forearms. The outside breeze had ruffled the midnight blackness of his hair. One lock of it hung waggishly over his forehead. He leaned against the door frame, hands in his pockets. His smile was crooked as he stared down at her.

"You're well enough to have on a fresh set of ruffles—you must be recovered. But you're barefoot. Starting to live dangerously? Just a little?"

Dinah fingered the ruffled yoke of her dress self-consciously. She curled her toes into the deep white carpet to hide them. "I—I thought you were Roscoe."

He shook his head and entered without her invitation. "Roscoe's too young to hang around the teacher's bedroom. He's in the music room. He and Mrs. Buttress are transcribing a few more songs. They hit if off famously. He reminds her of her middle son. He was singing. Did you hear him?"

"Yes," Dinah answered warily. Her hand, still resting at her throat, started to tremble again. She watched Mitch stroll to the huge bed, shrug, then sit on it. He leaned back, resting his weight on his elbow and studied her with disquieting candor.

"What do you want, anyway?" she demanded. "Why are you here? I don't remember asking you in."

"A mere oversight on your part, I'm sure," he said, green eyes moving from her small bare feet to the top of her blond head. "I only wanted to see how you are. Your light was on. I thought maybe you needed a mousetrap—or were lonely."

Normally Dinah would have bristled. But he had hit on exactly the right word to describe her this evening—*lonely.*

"Please forget about the mouse," she said unhappily. "I haven't reacted so strongly to one for years. It was just unfortunate, that's all."

"Really? I didn't mind. I liked saving you from the rampaging rodent. I hope you weren't up here brooding about it."

"I was reading," she fibbed blithely. "I'd completely forgotten about it."

"Hmm," he mused. He picked up the thick book from the night table, examined it and set it down again. "Doesn't look as if it's even been opened. Are you so superior you can read books without opening them?"

"Of course not," she replied. She stuck her hands into her pockets with a nonchalance she didn't feel. He was looking at her as if he could see her naked, both physically and mentally.

"If you're bored," he offered, his expression unreadable, "I thought you'd like to take a ride."

"What?" She tried to laugh. "Nashville by moonlight? Thanks—I saw enough of it by daylight."

To her consternation, he sat up straight, bent over and picked up her shoes, which had been peeping from under the bed. They were tiny, and he swung them by their straps from one finger. The gesture had a disturbing intimacy. "I doubt you saw much, really," he murmured. "I'd think you'd want to get out of this room for a while. Come here and put on your shoes. Then I'll show you where we're going to live."

Her fingers gripped the edge of the door, keeping it wide open for the sake of decency. "Where what?" she asked. "What did you say?"

He swung the small shoes provocatively. "I said come here, Cinderella. I want to see if these toy slippers really fit." He smiled at her. She froze, her breath stopping.

"Then I'll come and get you," he threatened genially. He rose, set the shoes on the night table and stalked purposefully toward Dinah. He swept her up into his arms so swiftly that she gasped. He strode back toward the bed and set her down on it, full length, just as swiftly. He sat down beside her and drew her bare feet onto his lap.

"What are you—"

He cut her off. "I asked you twice to put your shoes on. I don't ask anybody three times for something. I'm too impatient. I take action."

He grasped her left ankle in his right hand. With his other hand, he took her shoe from the table and slipped it on her foot. Dinah was unnaturally conscious of the sensuousness of the act—the firm warmth of his flesh against hers, the infinitely teasing slowness with which he slid the sandal onto her foot and fastened its complicated straps.

He released her left ankle, took her right and deftly slipped the other shoe on. He began fastening the straps. His touch made her legs tingle clear up to her thighs.

"Stop it," she hissed. "I can put on my own shoes. And the door is wide open. What if Roscoe comes by and sees this?"

"Sees what?" he asked. His fingers tightened, then released the last slim strap. Rising, he slid one arm under her legs, effortlessly shifting her weight so that her feet were on the floor again and she was standing. His movement was so fluid and surprising that she stared up at him in breathless surprise. His nearness was overwhelming. The dark silk of his shirt whispered slightly against the starched ruffles on her breast. His smile was elaborately casual. He stepped back. "Sees this?"

He bent and before she could protest, he took her hand and kissed the palm. His lips were warm against her skin. He turned her hand over and kissed every finger except the one with Dennis's ring. She fought to keep from shivering.

"What could be more respectful?" he asked, his mocking voice low.

"Just about anything," she said, snatching her hand back. She moved away from his dangerous nearness and went to stand by the open door. He sighed and crossed his arms. The motion made his square shoulders seem even wider. "Lord, you're a haughty little thing."

"Look," Dinah said, breathing hard. She wanted to defuse the situation; although his arrogance was colossal, she was in danger of succumbing to his air of sheer command. "Look, I'm not haughty. But I'm not used to men barging into my room, throwing me on my bed, dressing me, then presuming to—to—"

She held the door open more widely, inviting him to leave. He cocked an admonitory brow at her. "Tsk. Perhaps I should have thrown you on the bed and undressed you. Would that be better?"

"Hardly," she shot back. "Please leave. The way you act, the way you always act toward me, is disgraceful. I refuse to tolerate it."

"I'm acting like a normal, healthy man. You're obviously not used to it." He made no move to leave. Once more his gaze roamed her figure with proprietary interest.

"You're acting like a normal, healthy billy goat," she returned. "Leave. Go eat the laundry off the line or whatever it is billy goats do when they're not being . . . goatish."

Fine lines crinkled around his eyes. His smile had never seemed so lazy or insulting. "A sharp tongue, my prickly little thistle. Being rich didn't make you nice, did it?"

"You either," she accused.

"Come on," he urged, moving toward her. "Why argue? Let's go see where we're going to live." He draped one arm around her shoulders. The silk of his sleeves seemed to sweep her effortlessly to him.

"What do you mean—where we're going to live?" she breathed in bewilderment, unable to resist his embracing arm.

"Shh." He briefly put his finger to her lips. "You'll see. Come with me. The night is young. Almost as young and new as you. So put the bitter words aside and come. Because you want to. You know you do. Life's too short for pretending, Dinah."

She hesitated briefly, but she went. It was as if she had been waiting all her life to walk somewhere beside him, his arm around her in careless possession. *Where's he taking me?* one part of her mind asked. Another part replied, *It doesn't matter. It doesn't matter at all.*

THE NIGHT WAS BALMY, luminous with the shine of moon and stars, and in the distance the downtown lights of Nashville twinkled. Mitch's car, a black Excalibur, moved smoothly through the streets. He refused to tell her exactly where they were going, only that he was taking the long way.

"The long way?" Dinah asked, glancing at her watch. "It's past ten now. How long?"

"For starters," he replied, smiling at her in the moonlight, "I thought I'd take you by the temple of the Parthenon."

"The Parthenon?" objected Dinah, smoothing her breeze-tossed hair. "The Parthenon happens to be in Greece!"

"Only one's in Greece," Mitch returned. "This is Nashville, remember? Full of surprises."

If he was trying to be mysterious, he was succeeding admirably, Dinah thought. She had no idea of their final destination or what he meant by saying there was more than one Parthenon.

Briefly she stopped wondering as the car sped through downtown with its towering buildings. By night the heart of Nashville seemed enchanted, awash with a sense of quiet power, checkered with light and shadow.

Soon they were gliding down West End Avenue. Mitch slowed as they approached a great park. "There," he said with satisfaction. "You didn't believe me, did you?"

Dinah took in her breath audibly. Beyond the dark trees, she could see the columns and pediment of the Parthenon, immense and magnificent in the moonlight. Mitch pulled into the drive and switched off the car. She gazed in disbelief at the huge stone columns, the intricately carved friezes with their figures of gods and mortals. The structure's perfect proportions seemed both mammoth and ghostly.

"We're in Centennial Park," Mitch said softly, watching the wonder shining in her face. "This is the only full-size copy of the Parthenon in the world. We have temples of commerce downtown. But here we pay homage to the real thing."

"How strange," murmured Dinah, drinking in the carved figures that glimmered in the summer moonglow. "This must be how the real one looked—centuries and centuries ago."

"How it looked once, and will never be seen again. Except here," he answered. "People who've seen it only in pictures never imagine how huge it is. This is how it was before twenty-three centuries ravished it. And men spirited away its carvings for their museums." He paused. Casually he laid his arm along the back of her seat. "I hope you approve," he said sardonically. "Or are you one of those people who disdains copies—no matter how well intended?"

"It's beautiful," Dinah replied softly. "How wonderful—especially for the children—but in Nashville? I don't understand."

He started the car. "Nashville hasn't always been a center for country music," he informed her with a wry glance. "The music industry's relatively recent. I'll have you know, my Northern snowbird, that Nashville is also known as 'The Athens of the South'—it's a center of culture and learning. Hence, the great temple of Athens, the Parthenon."

Dinah smiled in spite of herself. "The Athens of the South? That's not the popular image."

"Popular images are usually incomplete and wrong," he said, nosing the car out of the park's stillness and heading east again. "The rest of the world may imagine this town as a honky-tonk, but Nashville is a true Southern belle—a complex, sophisticated and cultured lady. With just enough past and enough contradictions to keep her perpetually interesting."

"You sound like a man in love," she teased gently.

He cast her his scoffing look. "Close as I'm likely to get to being in love. At any rate, it's safer to love a city than a woman. A city never pretends to be faithful, the way some women do."

Dinah flinched. Did he think she was only pretending to be faithful to Dennis? Did he sense the contradictions that gripped her? "What makes Nashville so special to you?" she asked, trying to keep her tone light. "You don't sound like a Southerner. You sound Californian or Midwestern."

"Californian," he revealed. "Raised in L.A. Went to school in Chicago and London, then moved back to L.A. Now I'm a Southerner by choice. As for Nashville, I love her atmosphere, her paradoxes and her music. I love the electricity of her."

"What did you do before you came here?" she ventured, admiring his moon-silvered profile.

He all but ignored her question. "This. That. But this place felt like home from the first." He turned off the Murfreesboro Pike and onto a side street. "Nashville combines opposites. Modern industry and the grace of the antebellum South. And culture is serious business here. There are sixteen colleges and universities. Also a ballet, a symphony, an opera association and too many museums to count. It's a lot more than country music. If people bother to look."

Dinah snuggled more deeply into her seat. She felt slightly shamed. To her, Nashville had always meant hillbilly music, nothing more. Before she had come to Kakexia, the whole American South had been a hazy blur to her. She was guilty of provincialism, she knew. She supposed Mitch must think her a naive and snobbish fool. Perhaps that's why he was making a point of showing her Nashville's other side.

The Excalibur's headlights sliced through the night. Mitch had turned down another side road, lined with mimosa trees. A set of huge wrought-iron gates loomed, and beyond, a guard's headquarters. The entrance seemed to be to a private estate.

They stopped at the gates. Mitch spoke into a microphone set into a stone column beside the drive. "It's all right, Troutman. It's me, Mitch Carey. I'm showing the house to a friend."

Dinah watched as the gates obediently swung open. They entered and the car purred up the long ribbon of drive. Mitch waved hello to Troutman at his checkpoint, and the guard saluted back.

"What is this place?" Dinah asked, intrigued.

"It'll soon be at your disposal," he answered casually. He rounded another bend and before them, looming on a billowing rise of lawn, stood the most beautiful house Dinah had ever seen. It was a great octagon of pale pinkish brick, delicate in spite of its size, and ornamented with intricately trimmed white porches and lacy cornices. It seemed graceful and phantasmagoric in the blue night.

"Oh!" Dinah gasped. "Is that a real Southern mansion?"

"Yes and no," Mitch answered in his usual flippant tone. "It's a copy of one, of a villa really."

"Another copy?" She felt pleasantly bewildered. Nashville was becoming a shifting hall of mirrors, a place where illusion and reality were so richly mixed that she was losing her ability to distinguish the difference. "You're building it?"

He got out of the car and opened her door. "Almost." He laughed. "I'm finishing it. The original owner ran out of money. I hope to have it finished by the time the lease on the other place runs out. Care to take a look?"

"I'd love to," she answered, still marveling at the graceful lines of the villa. It seemed to float upon the night like an airy dream.

"It's been called a white elephant," Mitch admitted as he escorted her up the broad stairs to the filigreed veranda. "But the architecture's unique. The original in Mississippi was never completed because of the Civil War. I had to see the plans to find out how the house was intended to be when it was complete—perfected."

"It will be perfect," she said in awe. "I've never seen anything like it."

He unlocked the huge front doors with their curved tops. He felt inside for a switch, found it, and the entry hall was flooded in light. The floors were real marble, the color of pale smoke. To the right was the gracious sweep of a curved walnut staircase.

"Will you step into my parlor?" He looked down at her with a wicked quirk to his mouth. He had held her arm to guide her, and even so polite and impersonal a touch seemed to burn through the thin fabric of her sleeve.

"Not many lights are hooked up from here on out," he said, his lips brushing her hair as he spoke in a low voice. "We'll have to depend on the stars to guide us. And this." He reached out to a mantel for a brass candelabrum, then withdrew a lighter from his chest pocket and lit the three tall candles.

The flames threw a circle of golden light around them. Silently, they moved through the unfinished drawing room and into the parlor. Starshine and moonlight fell through the tall windows. The same rich gray marble of the hall entrance was beneath their feet. Gilded moldings glittered discreetly where the walls met the ceiling. Candlelight caught the prisms of the crystal chandelier and lit tiny multicolored fires within it.

"The chandelier's connected, but the workmen haven't cleaned up yet. Do you want to see it with the lights on?" he asked, his arm hard and warm against her shoulders.

"I like it this way better," she returned, reveling in the room's moon-washed mystery. He nodded and led her toward the arched windows that lined the north end of the room. "These overlook the lake, but the view is better from the porch. Or, as my snooty architect likes to call it, the veranda. Care to take a look?" He set the candelabrum on the floor and opened the outer door.

Bewitched, Dinah nodded and let him guide her outside. From the veranda's white balustrades she could see the lake stretching below them, stars reflecting on its dark surface. The tiny notes of night insects mingled, filling the air.

He stood behind her, winding both arms around her waist, resting his chin on her hair. "What do you think?"

The silk of his shirt made the feel of him incredibly seductive. His voice made her blood sing as happily as the night itself.

"It's lovely," she whispered. "Just lovely." She wasn't sure if she was talking about the house or about his nearness. If he were always like this, she thought, this gentle and strong, instead of challenging and derisive...

She wanted to enjoy the rarity of the moment, to close her eyes and lean her head back to rest against the silk-covered solidity of his chest.

"So." His voice, so close, had its familiar note of audacity. "Do you think we'll be happy here, Miss Priss? You and I, of course, the boy, who'll be like a son to us—until, thank God, he's old enough to move out?"

Living together? What was he thinking of? She broke from the pleasurable embrace and stepped away, wheeling to face him. "I have no idea what you're talking about." All she could think of was that for some unfathomable reason he was propositioning her, which showed precisely how little he respected her.

"In two months I'll be moving in." His voice was totally dispassionate. "If Roscoe's still here—and after listening to him tonight, I know he will be—then you'll be here. He needs you, you know. This is a dangerous business, Dinah. Unless he has someone to protect him, it can destroy him. You have to stay."

His hand stretched out, grazing the gold of her hair in an attempted caress. She stepped back again. She had no idea what game he was playing, but she had been foolish to let him lead her this far. "In two months Roscoe's contracts will be signed—or they won't. Either way, I have my own life to live. If Roscoe stays, somebody else will have to look out for him."

His attempt to touch her rebuffed, he shrugged and thrust his hands deep into the pockets of his slacks. "Nobody can do it with the passion you can. I saw you against Lucky Bucky today. You attacked him and backed him down by sheer force of character. He never listens to anybody, but he listened to you. I was impressed."

"Were you impressed when I nearly passed out afterward?" she asked bitterly. She wasn't proud of her showing this afternoon, and didn't believe he could be.

"No." His voice was clipped. He looked away. "I was concerned."

"I doubt that." She gave a short laugh of disbelief. "You seemed to think it was all quite funny."

He stared down at the star-sequined lake. "I know this is all hard on you..."

For once he didn't seem to be able to find the words. Dinah stood watching him. He looked suddenly angry, gazing off into the distance. He moved his shoulders impatiently.

"You're such a little thing," he said at last, grinding the words out. "Full of all the steel your great-grandfather was supposed to have, yet still scared of mice. What a paradox."

"I had a bad experience with a mouse when I was a child," she said defensively. "When I was five, my grandmother died. I didn't understand anything except that she was gone and I missed her. It was frightening. Then, right after the funeral, when the family gathered at my uncle's house, my cousin Dougal put a live mouse down my back. I got hysterical. I know it sounds neurotic, but it all got mixed up in my mind—death and losing someone I loved and mice. It sounds ridiculous, but I can't help it."

"It doesn't sound ridiculous," he contradicted. "And if I'd been there, I'd have cheerfully made mincemeat of your cousin Dougal. And I'd see that no one ever made you cry again." He paused. "You weren't very strong as a child—were you?"

His words stunned her. She'd never let anyone know about her youthful fragility. MacNeils weren't supposed to show any weakness, after all. Again she had the uneasy feeling his green eyes could cut through her soul, reading all secrets. She made no answer.

He turned to face her and set his hands lightly on her arms, but there was command in his touch. "Answer me, Dinah."

She felt her body tighten with defensiveness. How could his merest touch send such profound tremors through her? "I had some problems," she said noncommittally. "Minor problems. I'm perfectly fine—as long as there are no mice around."

"You should take care of yourself," he warned. His hands played over her, up to her shoulders, then back to her elbows. His voice was stern, yet peculiarly gentle. "Don't skip meals. Don't worry so much. You're worried all the time. I can tell. Oh, you hide it. You hide it beautifully. But not well enough to fool me. You're a beautiful contradiction, Dinah. Half prim child, half fiery woman. So spirited. But vulnerable. You're vulnerable—in spite of what you want anyone to think, aren't you?"

"No," she said, embarrassed, and this time it was she who turned away. She couldn't bear the teasing temptation of his casual caress. Her flesh felt both hot and cold where he had touched her. She stared off into a dark grove. "I'm not vulnerable. I'm surprisingly strong. I really am."

"He was a fool, your fiancé, to let you go off to that mining town. And to let you come here. Doesn't he know how hard you drive yourself? Doesn't he care about you at all?"

"Of course he cares about me. There's nothing to worry about—I said I'm fine."

"As long as you don't get overtired," he gibed. "Like today?"

"Yes," she answered crisply. The moonlight and his presence filled her with such strange excitement that she felt guilty, so she added, "And you've been rather tiring, Mr. Carey."

"So have you, Miss MacNeil," he parried. "But I think you have more on your mind than my boorishness. And Roscoe. In fact, I think Roscoe's right. That ring is draining your strength. It's too tight. You're strong, all right, but not strong enough to fight that. It's suffocating you."

Dinah sensed that he had moved close behind her again. If she turned, she knew he would take her in his arms. And if he took her in his arms, she knew she was lost. Lost, everything she stood for compromised, and she had known him slightly more than twenty-four hours. Sensible women didn't fall in love in the course of twenty-four hours. And a MacNeil would never, never catapult into such headlong folly.

"I happen to be very fond of my fiancé," she stated coldly, refusing to look at him.

"Then why are you here with me?" he asked. "And if he's in love with you, why in blazes did he let you get this far away from him?"

"Because." She stepped closer to the balustrade and gripped the railing. Her move to elude him didn't work. He stayed right behind her. She could feel his breath caressing the back of her neck. The heat of him seemed to penetrate her body. She spoke with tense desperation. "Because I felt I had a duty. Dennis and I are mature people. We realize sometimes responsibilities take precedence over pleasures. I've never confused love with 'romance,' Mr. Carey. Neither has Dennis. Our affection is strong enough to survive separations."

His laugh was low and impertinent. "What a perfect little hypocrite you are, Dinah. And what a fool your Dennis must be. If I loved you, I'd never let you far away for long. I'd guard you like a treasure."

Defiantly she kept her back to him. "Then it's a good thing you don't love me. Because I'm not a Dresden doll, and I don't belong to anyone. And never will."

"Dinah," he said gently. "You don't even belong to yourself yet. You're not sure who you are or what you want. That's what you came to Nashville to find out. And now you're afraid of what you're finding."

She nipped her lip sharply enough to hurt. "If you don't mind, I'd like to change the subject. I don't find myself all that interesting."

"All right. Let's talk about me. What did you find out about me today? And my offer to Roscoe? Every sort of dark secret?"

She took a deep breath. She had dreaded this moment, but now she was glad to retreat to the relative safety of discussing business. "I found out your offer's fair. That your advice is good. And that nobody knows much about you—good or bad."

"So are you going to drag this investigation on to the bitter end—all week long? Or are you satisfied that I'm not the devil incarnate?"

The jeer in his voice made her straighten her back even more stiffly. "I found out that your offer is the only one we're likely to get. Since you're Roscoe's only chance, I don't have much choice except to deal with you, and to be careful."

"Oh, you're good at that," he said disdainfully. "You're excellent at being careful. You've made it into a science."

His words stung because of their truth. She ignored the pain and kept her face turned to the darkness. "Then you'll know I mean it when I say I won't be here in two months. I'll be long gone. I'll make suitable arrangements for Roscoe, and then I'm going home. Where I belong."

"Do you?" he scoffed. "Belong there?"

"Of course." She bit her lip again.

"Maybe you do," he muttered harshly. "Maybe you have to live among the blue bloods to be happy. Well, I'll never be one of them. My money's too new. And slightly tainted."

"You probably find respectability boring," Dinah retorted out of hurt as much as anger. "Where I come from, people are concerned with manners—and breeding."

"Manners," he sneered. "These are my manners, Dinah. I'm showing them by not taking you in my arms and kissing you until you beg for mercy—and for more. But you're scared to death to have that cold blue Northern blood warmed." He tossed her a glittering look. "Especially by someone like me, eh?"

He stepped away from her. She felt the distance between them increase by more than physical space. "I'm not a snob," she said with quiet dignity.

"Come on," he said gruffly. "It's getting late and it was a waste of time bringing you here. I'll take you back. You need a decent night's sleep. I don't want you fainting again."

"I didn't faint and it won't happen again," she returned, sounding sharper than she meant to. "It's been years since anything like that happened to me."

"It happens when you wear tight rings," he murmured, bitterness darkening his voice. "But maybe it's that ring that makes you attractive, Dinah. A man always wants what he can't have. And who knows? If you weren't wearing it, I might not want you at all. Come on." She followed him into the parlor, where he retrieved the candelabrum. His brusk words stung, and Dinah was glad for the semidarkness so he couldn't see the burning of her face.

He drove her back to the house in silence, as if she weren't there at all. Dinah was relieved, yet disappointed, too. But what had she expected? She had built a barrier of ice between herself and Mitch. She had to. She belonged to New England and to her family traditions and, of course, to Dennis. She had always belonged to Dennis. And she always would. Everyone had said so.

CHAPTER SIX

DINAH AWOKE the next morning to the sound of ringing. Dazedly, she let her hand wander to the jeweled phone. She burrowed more snugly into the satin-covered pillow as she brought the receiver to her ear.

"Hello?"

"Dinah? It's Dennis, returning your call. And what is this nonsense that you've bitten off more than you can chew? I'm sure, sure, sure, you're going to be just fine, fine, fine."

"Dennis!" She sat up, feeling guilty and disoriented.

"I don't want to hear any chatter that you won't do splendidly in Nashville," Dennis said, pretending to be stern. "You mustn't be negative for another moment. It will make me cross."

She sat up. She ran her fingers through her tousled locks. "Dennis," she said again helplessly.

"I want to tell you once more that you can stay there as long as you need. Don't worry one bit about coming home until your job is done. You stay just as long as Rufus needs you."

"Rufus?" she asked. "You mean Roscoe?"

"Whoever," he chirped. "I'm just so proud that you've taken this poor, underprivileged boy under your capable wing."

"Roscoe's poor, but he's hardly underprivileged," Dinah said wryly. "And I'm not sure how capable my wing is."

"Negative thought! Negative thought! Don't think it! Put it out of your pretty head this minute!" he shrilled. "You can do anything you want. People said you shouldn't go to Kakexia, but I said, 'Piffle! She's as competent as can be! She'll do perfectly fine.' And you did."

"Who said I shouldn't go to Kakexia?" she asked suspiciously. Nobody had ever said such a thing to her face.

"Oh—people," Dennis answered vaguely. "Mother, for one. She said, 'Marry her right now, Dennis. You have money enough for the two of you. She doesn't have to do that silly year of public service. She's too delicate.'"

"I'm not delicate," Dinah protested. "I used to be, but I'm not anymore—"

"That's what I said," Dennis replied. "I said, 'Mother, Dinah used to have all that disgusting respiratory trouble but now she's strong as a veritable ox. She needs her own identity. Her own heritage. This is an age of liberation, Mother, of individuality.' That's what I said to her."

Somehow the conversation wasn't going as Dinah had hoped. "Dennis, this man we're staying with—he's a most upsetting man. He keeps suggesting—"

"Well, I say just don't let him upset you, that's what," Dennis advised. "No one can upset you unless you allow them. Put yourself on a higher mental plane."

"He's actually rather attractive," she said desperately. Dennis didn't seem to understand. "I find him rather attractive."

"Well, that's perfectly normal, isn't it?" piped Dennis. "I mean the world is full of attractive people. I wouldn't be so shallow as to tell you not to appreciate a handsome statue or painting. I won't say you shouldn't appreciate a handsome fellow. Goodness, no."

"Dennis," Dinah demanded, "what are you saying to me?"

"I'm just trying to be supportive," he replied. "If I can't be supportive, we wouldn't have much of a relationship, would we? I want to support your individuality, your personhood."

"Dennis," she said wearily, "my personhood is becoming very confused."

"Negative thought! Negative thought! Put it out of your mind! When I feel a negative thought coming on, I hum a little Mozart."

"Dennis, I'm trying to tell you that this man is behaving in a seductive fashion toward me!"

Dennis giggled. "Surely, Dinah," he said, "you must be imagining things. A seductive fashion? Toward you?"

"Well, yes, me. Why not me?" she demanded, hurt.

"You're not the type," he said with great assurance.

"I beg your pardon?"

"You're not the type. Of course," he mused, "he could be after your money."

"He has plenty of money, Dennis," she replied defensively. "Heaps of it." She didn't know where it came from, but she knew he had it.

"Hmm," he answered thoughtfully. "Well, he probably isn't being seductive toward you, then. You don't know much about that sort of thing, you know, Dinah. But if you find him attractive, well, certainly you should explore your own feelings."

"Dennis!" she cried, appalled. "What are you saying?"

"Just that you should explore the feelings of your own personhood. 'Know thyself.' It's the cornerstone of any workable philosophy."

"Are you telling me it's all right that I find another man attractive?"

"Of course," he said blithely. "I would not be very secure in my personhood if I said otherwise."

You may already have won the

MILLION DOLLAR
GRAND PRIZE!

IT'S FUN! IT'S FREE!
AND YOU COULD BE A
MILLIONAIRE!

Your unique Sweepstakes Entry Number appears on the Sweepstakes Entry Form. When you affix your Sweepstakes Entry Sticker to your Form, you're in the running, and you could be the $1,000,000.00 annuity Grand Prize Winner! That's $25,000.00 every year for up to 40 years!

AFFIX CASH AND
BONUS PRIZE STICKER

to your Sweepstakes Entry Form. If you have a winning number, you could collect any of 5,041 cash prizes. And we'll also enter you in special bonus prize drawings for a new Cadillac Coupe de Ville and the "Vacation of a Lifetime" (each prize worth $30,000.00)!

AFFIX FREE BOOKS
AND GIFTS STICKER

to take advantage of our Free Books/Free Gifts introduction to the Harlequin Reader Service. You'll get four brand new Harlequin Romance* novels, plus a handsome acrylic clock/calendar *and* a mystery gift, absolutely free!

NO PURCHASE NECESSARY!

Accepting free books and gifts places you under no obligation to buy anything! After receiving your free books, if you don't wish to receive any further volumes, write "cancel" on the shipping document and return it to us. There's no further obligation. But if you choose to remain a member of the Harlequin Reader Service, you'll receive eight more Harlequin Romance novels every month for just $1.99* each — 26 cents below the cover price, with no additional charge for shipping and handling! You can cancel at any time by dropping us a line, or by returning a shipment to us at our cost. Even if you cancel, your first four books, your digital clock/calendar, and your mystery gift are absolutely free — our way of thanking you for giving the Reader Service a try!

*Terms and prices subject to change.

SWEEPSTAKES RULES & REGULATIONS. NO PURCHASE NECESSARY.

Harlequin Reader Service® **Sweepstakes Entry Form**

This is your **unique** Sweepstakes Entry Number: 1A 897935

This could be your lucky day! If you have the winning number, you could be the Grand Prize Winner. To be eligible, *affix Sweepstakes Entry Sticker here!*

If you would like a chance to win the $35,000.00 prize, the $10,000.00 prize, or one of the many $5,000.00, $1,000.00, $500.00, or $5.00 prizes ... plus the Cadillac and the Vacation of a Lifetime, *affix Cash and Bonus Prize Sticker here!*

To receive free books and gifts with no obligation to buy, as explained in the advertisement, *affix the Free Books and Gifts Sticker here!*

118 CIH FAVD

Please enter me in the sweepstakes and tell me if I've won the $1,000,000.00 Grand Prize! Also tell me if I've won any other cash prize, or the car, or the vacation prize. And ship me the free books and gifts I've requested with the sticker above. Entering the sweepstakes costs me nothing and places me under no obligation to buy! (If you do not wish to receive free books and gifts, do not affix the FREE BOOKS and GIFTS sticker.)

YOUR NAME   PLEASE PRINT

ADDRESS   APT. #

CITY   STATE   ZIP

Offer limited to one per household and not valid for current Harlequin Romance subscribers.

P.O. Box 1867, Buffalo, NY 14269-1867.

DETACH ALONG DOTTED LINE

PRINTED IN U.S.A

DETACH ALONG DOTTED LINE

BUSINESS REPLY MAIL

FIRST CLASS   PERMIT NO. 717   BUFFALO, NY

POSTAGE WILL BE PAID BY ADDRESSEE

HARLEQUIN READER SERVICE®
MILLION DOLLAR SWEEPSTAKES
901 Fuhrmann Blvd.
P.O. Box 1867
Buffalo, NY 14240-9952

NO POSTAGE
NECESSARY
IF MAILED
IN THE
UNITED STATES

"Dennis," she returned slowly, "I guess all I can say is thank you for being secure in your personhood."

"You're welcome," he replied. Generosity dripped from his voice.

When Dinah hung up, she pulled the lace-edged pillow to her and hugged it. She felt slightly ill. She looked at the enormous diamond on her hand. It seemed to mock her.

Everything was terrifyingly clear now. She felt as if she had awakened from a dream that had lasted years. She didn't love Dennis. She never had. He had been a friend, that was all, a friend she had outgrown. What's more, Dennis didn't love her. He was glad she had gone to Kakexia, glad she had come to Nashville. If he were honest, he probably felt as trapped by their engagement as she did.

She wanted to take the ring and hurl it across the big room. No, she thought, still feeling half-sick. That would be childish. And if she took it off, Mitch Carey would think it was because of him. She couldn't take it off. Not until she was home and could hand it back to Dennis in person.

She rose and went to the closet. She wanted to find something that hadn't a single ruffle or piece of lace on it.

DINAH SAT on the patio, drinking coffee. She wore a demure cotton dress of glen plaid with a high neck. Roscoe sat beside her, wolfing down croissants and sausages. His white hat kept falling over his eyes.

"Roscoe," she murmured grimly, "the time has come to speak of table manners."

"Yes, ma'am," Roscoe said obediently and reached for a Danish pastry.

"I know your mother didn't raise you to gobble that way. Slow down. Chew, don't gulp."

"Yes, ma'am," replied Roscoe and actually slowed a bit.

"Ah, every inch the schoolteacher," said Mitch Carey. "Even at breakfast. How daunting."

She whipped her head around. He had appeared behind them. His thick black hair gleamed in the morning sunlight. He wore thigh-hugging faded jeans and a white Greek sailor shirt that laced rather than buttoned.

He pulled out one of the wrought-iron chairs and sat down. The bearded servant materialized, swiftly laying another place for Mitch and pouring his coffee.

Mitch thanked him and took a leisurely sip. "Well, Roscoe, how do you and Miss MacNeil plan to spend the day?"

"I don't know, sir," Roscoe said, and looked expectantly at Dinah.

"Will she be playing agent again and trying to find you a better offer than mine?"

"Don't know, sir," Roscoe repeated, embarrassed.

"I've learned my lesson, Mr. Carey," Dinah admitted reluctantly. "I guess we're at your disposal."

"A pity I haven't time for you," he returned cheerfully. But when he saw the lost expression on Roscoe's face, he quickly added, "Don't worry, m'boy. Miss MacNeil said she'd be keeping you occupied most of the time until Friday, and I arranged my schedule accordingly. I'd like to see you this afternoon at four again. But the rest of the day is yours. See Nashville. Get acquainted with it."

Roscoe grinned in relief. "Yessir. I'd like to see Elvis Presley's gold Cadillac, sir."

"Indeed," Mitch said with conviction. "Everyone who comes to Nashville should see Elvis's gold Cadillac. You'll find it at the Country Music Hall of Fame. At Music Square East."

Dinah didn't find the idea of a gold Cadillac enticing, but Mitch's presence made her so prickly and uncomfortable that she wanted to escape. She glanced at her watch. "Then

I suppose we should get an early start," she said brightly and started to rise.

Mitch reached out and grasped her wrist, forcing her, gently but firmly, to sit again.

"I don't think you've learned your lesson, Miss Mac-Neil," he said with a smile. "At least not all of it."

"What do you mean?" she asked, bewildered by his touch. He kept hold of her wrist, stroking it slowly.

"Your plate is spotless," he pointed out. "You haven't eaten anything, have you?"

"I'm not hungry," she protested. She wasn't. She still felt a bit unwell from her realizations about Dennis.

"Eat," he ordered implacably. She was relieved when he took his hand from her wrist but dismayed when he heaped a golden mound of eggs onto her plate. He broke open a warm croissant and spread it thickly with butter for her. "Eat," he repeated, handing it to her.

In chagrin, she forced herself to bite into the soft roll. She looked at him with resentment, which he cheerfully ignored.

He didn't take his bold yet unreadable gaze from her. His impact on her was just as potent in sunlight as it had been by moonlight. He frightened her. He made too many new ideas, new sensations course through her. In panic, she hurried to finish her food.

Mitch cocked an eyebrow and gave a superior smile at her haste. "Now, now," he said lazily. "I'm sure your mother didn't raise you to gobble. Chew, don't gulp."

DINAH STARED at Elvis Presley's gold Cadillac. It sat behind a velvet rope in all its glory. Roscoe gaped at it. The huge car was equipped with a refrigerator, a television and a soda fountain.

"Mercy doo-wah!" Roscoe murmured in awe. "If I ever get rich, I'm gonna buy my mama a car just like that."

Dinah started to say that surely Vesta would prefer something more sensible but caught herself. Let the boy have his dreams, she thought. Besides, she was beginning to realize that the world of country music did not believe in understatement. Its taste was flamboyant and proud of it.

She turned away from the car, suddenly feeling alone and lost. Roscoe understood this museum far better than she did. He knew every name enshrined within a star in the lobby; he recognized the photographs; he revered the artifacts. She was so ignorant, she thought. How would she ever be able to guide him?

She turned back to him on impulse. "Roscoe," she said, laying her hand on his thin arm. "I don't know much about your music at all. Can you teach me?"

He faced her, his mouth slightly open. "Me? Teach you?"

"Yes," she said earnestly, looking up at him. "Please."

He took off his hat. His brown hair was slightly mussed. "Why, I'd be proud to," he said solemnly. "Truly proud."

He put on his hat and swallowed hard. "As far as I'm concerned, the music really came into its own with a singer named Hank Williams. It's like he gave Nashville its heart and its soul. He was the greatest country singer ever. But he died young. So young. Still, he changed the music forever. He made it great."

She smiled proudly at his eloquence. She admitted again to herself how fond she was of him. He was that rarest of creatures, a born gentleman. And, she realized with a new sense of responsibility, it was her job to keep him that way.

Roscoe was not so overwhelmed by the sights that he forgot his duties. As soon as he saw that noon approached, he told Dinah she had to eat. To avoid the crush of tourists they ducked into a tiny restaurant off the beaten track.

They sat in a cramped booth, waiting for their sandwiches. Roscoe squinted at a map he had picked up. Dinah was glad she'd somehow managed to still have enough presence of mind after her conversation with Dennis to make Roscoe's appointments with the optometrist and dentist.

"We'll go see the *General Jackson*," he muttered, poring over the print. "That's a real paddlewheel showboat. And the Grand Ole Opry buildin'. And the recordin' studios on Division Street..."

"If Mitch Carey wants her, he'll get her," a man's voice said.

Dinah straightened, no longer listening to Roscoe. The voices coming from the next booth arrested her attention.

"How do you know?" scoffed a woman's voice.

"Because he's gotten everything else he's wanted," said the man. "I've been watching him since he hit town. He's a different breed of cat than his brother. Altogether different. He knows what he's doing. If he wants Vonda, he'll get her."

"Vonda's too big a star," the woman argued. "Why would she break a contract to throw in with somebody like Mitch Carey? He hasn't produced a single record yet."

"She'll do it because he's got the guts to offer her what nobody else will—a chance to do things her way."

"She's crazy if she changes her act," the woman protested. "She's got a sure thing going. Why fool with it?"

"Because maybe she'd like to think of herself as an artist, for a change, not a product."

"Artist!" laughed the woman. "Artist, my foot. She's got a great shape and all that gorgeous blond hair. She's a beauty—but an artist? Hardly."

"You remember her early records?" the man asked quietly. "Before her stuff got all slick and commercial?"

"She was interesting," the woman admitted. "But that's not the Vonda the public wants. She's got an image that's worth a million dollars. I can't see her changing it for the sake of 'artistic freedom.' If she goes with Mitch Carey, she'll go for one reason."

"What's that?"

"Because she wants Mitch Carey, that's why. They're two of a kind. They know what they want when they see it. And when they see it, they go after it. And when they go after it, they get it. And she's going after him."

"How do you know?" the man challenged.

"Because she was staying with him at the mansion. At Bobby's mansion. Until that kid came in. That kid that Carey's signed up."

"What about this kid?" the man questioned. "Who is he?"

"I don't remember his name," the woman answered, "but he's supposed to be incredible. A natural. A complete original. The only problem is he has some woman watching out for him who's really hard to take. A real pain. Lucky Bucky says Carey's going to take the starch out of her, though—he'll cut her down to size and leave her bleeding, begging for mercy—"

Dinah had heard enough. She stood abruptly and marched to the jukebox. She was almost shaking with anger and humiliation. She fed all her quarters into the machine and punched buttons at random.

People who eavesdrop, she thought bitterly, *shouldn't complain about what they hear.* So that was Mitch Carey's game, was it? Cut her down and leave her begging for mercy. She should have known. A man like him would see someone like her as only a challenge, an opponent to humble. It explained his pretended interest in her. It also sickened her. And who, she wondered, bleakly, was Vonda, the beautiful woman in whom he was truly interested?

The music of the jukebox blared, wailing strongly about cheating hearts and love gone wrong.

By four o'clock, Dinah felt she had walked through half of Nashville. Trying to keep herself distracted, she had questioned Roscoe about country music until her head spun with names, trends, facts. But, efficient as usual, she had also managed a short shopping session for Roscoe, who was now resplendent in new jeans, a peach-colored cowboy shirt and shiny brown boots. He had, however, refused to listen to her pleas to replace his lucky hat with one that fit.

As they made their way to Diamond Horseshoe, Roscoe was burdened with packages, and his hat was, as usual, falling over his eyes. Dinah noticed a workman attaching a metal plaque to the cornerstone of Mitch's building. Diamond Horseshoe Records, it read, Built on the Vision of Bobby Carey. She glanced at it in puzzlement. What a complicated man Mitch was, she mused unhappily, determined to erect some kind of monument to his brother's brief and reckless life. The gesture surprised and confused her.

Inside, Mrs. Buttress, calm amid the chaos of builders, had donned her shower hat once more to protect her hair from the falling plaster dust. Like a sergeant at arms, she briskly marched the two of them into Mitch's office.

Lucky Bucky, in all his immensity, was seated by the window. He was blinding in electric blue, and he did not bother to rise when Dinah entered. He glared at her sulkily.

"Roscoe," Mitch said. "You're quite natty. Miss MacNeil has decked you out admirably. My compliments, Miss MacNeil. Remind me to reimburse you." He flashed her his mocking white smile.

"There'll be no need," she answered matter-of-factly. "Roscoe will do it himself when you pay him for these three weeks."

"Then I'll have Mrs. Buttress make out the check immediately," he answered. "Please—be seated."

"He ought to get rid of that dad-blamed hat," muttered Lucky Bucky, eyeing Roscoe critically. "Looks like hell."

"It's Roscoe's hat and he likes it," Dinah said between her teeth. She didn't like the hat herself, but she wouldn't allow Lucky Bucky to be rude.

"It still looks awful," Bucky grumbled, flicking an imaginary speck from his blue-clad leg.

"Shall we get down to business?" Mitch asked sarcastically. "Or shall we sit and discuss Roscoe's hat?"

Bucky looked even sulkier, and Roscoe shifted uncomfortably in his chair. Dinah tried to steel herself against Mitch's charm and hated herself for wondering, for the hundredth time that afternoon, who Vonda was. "Let's talk business," she said.

"Fine. I've lined up musicians for Roscoe's demo. I want him to rehearse all next week. It's not the usual procedure, but it's what I want. If they work out, they may become his permanent backup band. All right?"

"How many musicians? On what instruments?" Dinah asked. Roscoe's teachings hadn't fallen on deaf ears. She felt she could at least ask the right questions.

Mitch gave her a measuring look. She had surprised him. "Electric guitar, electric bass, drums and fiddle. I want the sound behind him to be very basic."

Dinah glanced at Roscoe. She saw the approval on his face. She knew he liked his music uncluttered. He had told her he'd hoped for just such a sound.

She nodded briskly. "It's agreeable to us."

Roscoe nodded, too.

Mitch gave her another long look. "I want four songs on the tapes. Three that Roscoe's written, the ones we talked about last night—" he glanced at the boy, then back at Dinah "—and one Hank Williams, Sr., song. He's got a lot of the same purity that Williams had. Comparisons are bound to be made. Let's bring it right out front from the beginning."

Dinah looked to Roscoe again and saw him swallow nervously. She knew that a comparison to Hank Williams was the highest of compliments and Roscoe would not believe it.

"I don't know that I ought to do any song of his," Roscoe said hesitantly. "I don't know that I'd be fittin'—that I'd have the right to—you know?"

She reached out and put her fingers lightly on his shoulder. "You can do it," she said confidently.

She locked eyes with Mitch. "He'll try."

She saw Roscoe swallow again. "It'll be all right," she told the boy softly. "If it doesn't work out, we can change it."

"Yes, ma'am," he said humbly.

"And—" Mitch sighed, turning to Lucky Bucky "—Bucky's been working on the image that Roscoe will project. He assures me he has some interesting ideas."

"Great minds think alike," Bucky announced. "It's crossed my thoughts more than once that Roscoe's gonna be compared to Williams. I agree. Confront the comparisons immediately. After all, Nashville's been waitin' nearly forty years for another Williams. But I say, don't just confront the similarities—exploit them!"

Mitch, who had been toying with a pencil, stopped and watched Lucky Bucky carefully. Dinah went still with apprehension. She heard Roscoe's nervous gulp.

"I say," Lucky Bucky continued, with all the zeal of a salesman, "we dress him like Williams. We bill him as the new Williams. Williams's band was the Cowboy Drifters. We call Roscoe's band the Ghost Drifters, like the whole bunch, including Roscoe, is the reincarnation of the originals. We plant stories in the tabloids that he even believes he's the reincarnation of Williams. I can see our slogan now: Hank Lives Again.''

The silence that greeted the end of Lucky Bucky's speech was absolute and ominous. Mitch's face was carefully blank. Roscoe, whom Dinah had never seen truly angry, was turning red and breathing hard. His hands were clenched into bony fists.

"Well?" asked Lucky Bucky, waiting for the praise to begin pouring out.

"I'm speechless," Mitch said, his expression still unreadable.

Roscoe was making a small choking noise deep within his throat. Finally he managed to utter a single, strangled word: "No!"

Lucky Bucky looked at the boy with disdain. "What do you mean no, you ignoramus? I'm the promoter. What do you know? Will you listen for once? This is a million-dollar idea—a commercial dream. If you turn down this idea, you hick, you're dumber than—"

Both Lucky Bucky and Roscoe had got to their feet. Dinah sprang up and stood between them. "That kid don't know nothin'," the big man huffed angrily. "That kid should not be allowed to tell me no. That kid should learn to listen to his betters—"

"Watch your tone!" she warned. She turned, her eyes flashing to Mitch. "Aren't you going to say something?" she demanded.

"I imagine you'll think of what to say," Mitch replied laconically. He leaned his chin on his fist and watched the unfolding scene with scientific interest.

Lucky Bucky towered before Dinah, his fat face trembling with indignation. He was six feet three inches and weighed close to three hundred pounds. Roscoe stood right behind her, breathing hard. He was nearly six feet, and weighed about one hundred and thirty. Dinah felt tiny between them, but she refused to back down.

"Step back," she ordered Roscoe, and something in her voice made him obey.

"And you," she said, shaking her finger up in Lucky Bucky's face, "sit down and stop trying to intimidate the boy. If you want to pick on somebody, pick on me."

"If I wasn't a gentlemen, I would squash you like a bug," Bucky sneered, but the fire in Dinah's eyes made him take a step backward. "Fortunately for you," he said, "I don't fight with women." He sat down as if the whole situation were not worthy of his notice.

Dinah remained standing. She glared down at him. "You are going to fight with a woman, Mr. Williston, and I am the woman. Your 'idea' not only displeases my client, it offends him. You'll not exploit the memory of a dead man, a legend in your industry, simply for the sake of money. It's irreverent, it's tasteless and it's ghoulish. We want no part of it."

"Dang it!" Bucky shouted. He snatched off his Stetson and flung it to the ground. "I think my head clear to the bone comin' up with million-dollar ideas, and you and this kid throw them back in my face! I'm gettin' sick of it! What do either of you know?"

Dinah turned to Roscoe, who still glared indignantly at Lucky Bucky. "Sit down, Roscoe," she said quietly. "Please." Roscoe sat. She stole a glance at Mitch, who was examining the point of his pencil with great interest. He wasn't going to help her at all.

Lucky Bucky looked to Mitch for support. "Are you gonna let her get away with this?" he demanded. "Make her behave, durn it."

Mitch cast him a brief, cool glance. "I can't make her behave, Bucky. She has a mind of her own."

"You like my idea, don't you?" Bucky almost whined. "You can see the commercial potential, can't you? This may be the best idea I've ever had."

"As your ideas go, Bucky, I'd say it's one of your most unique. But the artist—and his lovely representative here—" he gestured toward Dinah "—don't like it. I guess you'll have to come up with something else. Maybe, since you find them so difficult, you should ask them what they'd like."

Lucky Bucky looked at Dinah with narrowed eyes. "She ain't difficult," he growled, his jowls shaking. "She's impossible. She's a spoiled snob and she's makin' the kid into one, too. I'm an artist. They have violated my artistic integrity. I refuse to work with them."

He stood, bent over to pick up his Stetson and jammed it on his head. "I'm sorry, Mr. Carey," he said pompously. "Call me when you find people who appreciate my talents." He walked out the door, stamping so emphatically that his weight shook the floor.

Roscoe looked after him with a pale face. He looked up at Dinah. "I don't care," he said. "I don't care if I get sent home. I ain't gonna pretend to be no ghost. I'm just me, that's all I am."

"It's all right," Mitch said reassuringly. He rose and moved to the boy, putting his hand on his shoulder. "You're right. He was wrong. I'm not angry. I'm glad he's gone."

Mitch turned to Dinah, smiling down at her ironically. "Sit down," he murmured. "You're shaking."

Dinah wasn't sure if she was shaking from the encounter with Lucky Bucky or her indignation toward Mitch, but she quickly sank back into her chair. "You could have helped," she said, looking up at him accusingly.

"It's cleaner the way it happened," he replied lazily. He sat on the edge of his desk. "If I tell him he's not going to be Roscoe's promoter, he'll yell 'breach of contract' and try to sue me. He's famous for tricks like that. But he's the one who walked out. In short, he's burnt his bridges behind him."

Dinah's head swam in confusion. Mitch looked as smug as a green-eyed cat who'd just dined on the plumpest of canaries. She had a rising suspicion that she'd been used, and quite cleverly, too. But she didn't have time to pursue the thought.

"So," he said, watching her small form with interest as she sagged against the big chair. "What do you think Roscoe's image should be? How should he be presented to the public?"

Dinah looked into his taunting face, then at Roscoe, who sat, silent and ill at ease. She thought she knew the boy well enough to speak for him, to say what he was afraid to say himself. "What's wrong with the way he looks right now?" she asked, and was grateful to see Roscoe relax. "Why does he have to dress up strangely or act like somebody else?" she asked. "He looks fine just as he is—Western clothes that are comfortable and well made. What's wrong with that?"

"Not a thing," Mitch answered, crossing his arms. "It's what I hoped you'd say. And what should the backup band be called?"

Dinah, suddenly exhausted, felt drained. "Roscoe should decide that," she said wearily. "It'll be his band."

"Then what would you like to call them, m'boy?" Mitch asked, his face more kindly as he turned to Roscoe.

"I reckon I'd have to think about it," Roscoe replied, frowning slightly. "I mean, I ain't even heard 'em yet."

"A wise answer." Mitch smiled. He moved to the window and sat on the sill. "A thoughtful answer. You must have had some very fine teachers in school."

"Yessir," Roscoe said, glancing shyly at Dinah. "I did, sir."

"I'll let the two of you go. And by the way, just so you won't be surprised, there'll be company for dinner tonight. But it won't be formal."

Dinah and Roscoe rose and she started to follow the boy out the door. But Mitch stepped toward her and drew her back. "I want to see you alone a moment," he murmured, his voice husky.

Roscoe exited, and as the door swung shut, Dinah stared up at Mitch in helpless perplexity. Her emotions had been battered and torn all day long. She didn't feel she had the strength to fight or resist Mitch anymore.

He pulled her to him gently but forcefully. "I just want to tell you," he said, his voice low, "that you were magnificent."

"I—" Dinah breathed, then could not finish the sentence. She was lost in the pale emerald mystery of his eyes.

"Magnificent," he repeated, pulling her nearer. She felt the powerful flexing of the muscles in his arms, the hypnotic maleness of him. He bent over her, lowering his lips to hers. The urgent heat of his mouth stunned her, as did his hands moving expertly over her rib cage, drawing her body still closer to his, so that her breasts were crushed by the hard wall of his chest.

For an endless moment his mouth explored hers with expertise and passion. He had lifted her until she was standing on her tiptoes, yet she strained to rise even higher, as if he could make her fly, and the two of them could soar away on this kiss.

She moaned her pleasure ever so slightly as she felt his tongue glide over her trembling lips to pillage her inner sweetness. Her own tongue answered, tasting him with blissful intimacy. When her arms crept shyly around his neck, he took in his breath harshly and kissed her with an intensity that again made her feel that she was flying, locked in his taut arms. She knew that the feeling sweeping through her, in wave after hot dark wave, was desire.

His feverish kisses bore her, dizzy, to new levels of awareness and need. Never had a man made her feel this way. His lips told her of his hunger, and hers answered, begging him to teach her more about the fiery emotions coursing through her.

Then, abruptly, he drew back so slightly that his mouth barely touched hers. She could feel his breath on her tingling lips when he spoke. "If I don't stop this," he whispered, his hands moving over her with increasing urgency, "I'll be carrying you back to that couch in the inner office. And how would we explain that to your darling fiancé whom you love so well?"

His words brought her back to herself with a painful jolt. She was glad, though, that he still held her, for her knees were trembling too much to bear her weight. He drew back a few inches farther. He stared down at the vulnerability of her mouth, the puzzled, yearning pain in her eyes, and his expression softened. "Poor Dinah," he scoffed gently. "So sophisticated, yet so unworldly. So educated, yet so innocent. So full of principles, but so unsure of who you really are and what you really want."

The truth hurt, and she tried to deny it. "I know who I am and I know what I want," she lied.

"Then why are you so frightened of feeling, Dinah?" he asked softly. "And of me?"

She shook her head in confusion, avoiding his eyes. She feared him precisely because of what he made her feel, of what he had made her feel from the moment she had seen him. The intensity of her emotions kept growing, becoming increasingly terrifying and foreign to her. Yet from everything she knew, she dared not trust this man. "I—I have to go—" she stammered. "Roscoe's waiting."

He released her with a swiftness that bordered on the contemptuous. "We'll finish this discussion another time," he muttered. "You have to get back to your precious charge and I have work to do. I'll see you at supper. Remember, company's coming, so you might warn Roscoe to curb his usual eating habits and refrain from eating the tablecloth."

She stepped away from him gingerly. She ran her hand over her short hair, smoothing it. She caught a glimpse of herself in a mirror on the wall and was shocked by how pink her cheeks were, how her lips were bare of lipstick and swollen with the demands of his kiss.

Years of keeping careful control of herself came to her rescue. She erected a brittle facade of capability. She stepped to the mirror and reapplied her lipstick quickly and expertly. "Roscoe has a healthy appetite," she said coolly. "It's normal in boys his age."

"I have a healthy appetite myself," he said significantly. "It's normal in men my age."

Dinah shivered, for she knew precisely what he was talking about. She pretended to disregard him as she blotted her pink lipstick on a tissue, folded it and discarded it neatly.

"Who's coming this evening, if I may ask?" she queried, facing him again, her old defenses all intact.

He shrugged moodily. "Nobody you'd know," he muttered. He was staring with disturbing fixity at her lips.

"Another of my artists. Vonda Rainy. She'll be signing with me soon."

Dinah calmly disguised the fact that the name made her spirits sink like a stone. "Ah," she said calmly. "How nice. We'll see the two of you then." She turned smartly on her heel and left his office.

On the way home she gave Roscoe a tactful lecture on table manners, but behind her brisk pose, she ached all over. After all she'd been through that day, she was in no mood to sit down to supper with the woman Mitch really wanted. Dinah wondered bitterly how the man could try to seduce her one moment, then flaunt another of his conquests before her the next. Because he was a ruthless and unethical beast, she decided. And because he had vowed to cut her down to size.

Her mood darkened further when she told Roscoe that the evening's guest would be Vonda Rainy. He rolled his eyes and feigned that his heart was failing. "Glory!" he moaned in pleasurable pain. "Vonda Rainy?"

"Do you mind explaining your reaction? I don't know anything about her."

"She's only the most beautiful woman in Nashville," Roscoe said in true awe. "Maybe in the whole world. Maybe in the whole entire great big universe."

"Oh," Dinah said tonelessly. And she felt worse than before.

CHAPTER SEVEN

VONDA RAINY, it turned out, probably *was* the most beautiful woman in Nashville. She arrived in a chauffeured limousine, and she wore curve-hugging blue jeans and Western boots of beautiful white leather. Her gauzy pink top had billowing sleeves and was tucked into the jeans and cinched with a wide belt that emphasized her tiny waist and the fullness of her breasts and hips. Her belt buckle blazed with rhinestones and her diamond earrings were the showiest that Dinah had ever seen.

The woman did not so much walk into the big house as skip and bounce. She had an unbelievable wealth of strawberry-blond hair that cascaded halfway to her waist. Her eyes were enormous, brown and heavily made up. Her lashes seemed half an inch long. She was fully six inches taller than Dinah, and next to her Dinah felt small, drab, boring and out of place.

Vonda kissed Mitch heartily on the cheek, then kissed a blushing Roscoe, saying she knew he was going to be a big success. She pumped Dinah's hand and proclaimed she was pleased to meet her.

Dinah stood, wearing her basic black dress and no jewelry except her ring, feeling plainer every moment. It would be easier, she thought guiltily, if she could dislike her. But the woman was too full of life, too outgoing and bursting with nervous energy, to dislike.

After supper, they retired to the living room, and Vonda asked Mitch for a guitar. She wanted to sing with Roscoe. Mitch went to the music room himself, as if he knew precisely which instrument Vonda needed and didn't trust a servant to bear it to her. Roscoe practically ran upstairs for his own guitar.

"Quite a boy," Vonda said. She was sitting on the floor, long legs crossed, drinking a glass of champagne. Dinah perched on the edge of her chair, her knees together and ankles crossed. She felt as prim as a maiden aunt. She wished she, too, were wearing jeans and sitting with careless ease on the carpet.

"Yes," she agreed. "Wait till you hear him sing."

"I've heard him!" Vonda exclaimed, her dark eyes widening. She stared over the rim of her champagne glass at Dinah. "Didn't Mitch tell you? I found him."

"You what?" Dinah asked, setting down her champagne. Her blue gaze locked with Vonda's surprised brown one. "I thought Lucky Bucky found him."

"Nope," the other woman stated simply. "Mitch sent Lucky Bucky to check him out. But I found him. I heard him and two of his friends at a county fair in Kentucky. I said to myself, 'This kid has got it.' And I came back and told Mitch because I knew he was the one person smart enough to listen. He didn't tell you?"

"No," Dinah said, shaking her head. Mitch hadn't told her anything at all about Vonda Rainy, she thought unhappily.

Vonda tossed her shimmering reddish-blond waves. "Well, I told him not to tell the kid. I didn't want Roscoe getting all sloppy and grateful. But I thought he'd probably tell you. You bein' his guardian and all."

"But how—" Dinah struggled to clear her confused thoughts "—how could you have been there and Roscoe not

have seen you? He thinks you're wonderful. I'm sure he
would have recognized you."

"Simple, honey," Vonda said with a laugh. "I needed a
vacation from being me, know what I mean? I put on a
brown wig, I took off my makeup, and went on a vacation
disguised as a normal person. I got kin in Kentucky. I'd
stopped off to see them. My nephew raised a pig that took
a blue ribbon at the fair, and course I had to go see that. So
I discovered Roscoe because of a pig, and that's a fact.
Don't tell me life ain't strange." She laughed again, deep in
her throat.

Dinah had to smile, too. Vonda sobered. She looked
suddenly uncomfortable. "Mitch, he's closemouthed. He's
hard to read. He might not have told you I lived here for a
while. This is a town where news gets around, and you'll
hear it sooner or later. I just want you to know there was
nothing to it—him and me. We're just friends, that's all.
Don't misunderstand."

"Oh," Dinah responded out of nervous politeness. "Of
course not. Not at all."

"Good," murmured Vonda. "There was nothing to it.
Nothing between us. It shouldn't be interesting to anybody
at all. But people—they talk. They like to talk. So now
they're talkin' about us. Ignore it." Her face had a shut-
tered, private look as if she were hiding something. Mo-
mentarily the dark eyes stared off into some private world.
Then she turned her charm back on. "So is Mitch treating
you all right?" she asked cheerfully. "He can be such a
devil."

"All of Nashville has treated us well," Dinah replied with
an evasiveness she found uncomfortable. Unlike Vonda, she
was not a performer and no expert at hiding powerful emotions.

For the rest of the evening, she discreetly watched Vonda and Mitch. She saw how Vonda looked at him with an expression that seemed both fond and haunted. And Mitch showed Vonda a kindness and regard that Dinah envied. Toward Dinah he was courteous but distant.

Roscoe alone seemed oblivious to the complex emotions in the room. He was caught up in his music. He sang, at first nervously, then with growing confidence and spirit.

"Woo!" Vonda exclaimed, when he had finished one especially stirring ballad. "Are you good or what, boy? Let me sing with you. Do you know 'Sweet Sixteen'—the one that goes 'I love you as I never loved before'?"

Roscoe nodded. Vonda, taking the lead on her guitar, began, and Roscoe joined her. Their voices blended together with an almost eerie perfection. Dinah had never before heard Roscoe sing with anyone who had a fraction of his talent. The result took her breath away and she listened entranced.

> I loved you as I've never loved before,
> Since first I saw you on the village green.
> Come to me in my dreams of love adored—
> I love as I loved you
> When you were sweet—
> When you were sweet sixteen.

For some reason, tears welled in Dinah's eyes. The song was the clear and uncomplicated essence of lasting love. She realized that somehow it said exactly what she felt for Mitch. *I love you as I've never loved before.* The thought startled her.

Yet it was ridiculous, she told herself sternly. She and Mitch were not sweet sixteen. It was Dennis, not Mitch, that she had known when she was that young, and Dennis was completely wrong for her. And Mitch belonged to the beautiful woman who sat by his feet.

As Vonda and Roscoe reached the last notes, Dinah felt Mitch's eyes on her. He studied her with a disconcerting intensity, his face masked, his eyes unfathomable. She sat, pale, unable to take her gaze from his. Her lips parted involuntarily.

His stare focused on that almost imperceptible movement, dwelling boldly on her mouth. The song ended. Silence swelled the air.

Mitch glanced ironically at the great diamond winking on Dinah's hand, gave her a cold half smile and turned his attention back to Roscoe and Vonda. Dinah's chest knotted with pain and longing.

Vonda seemed deeply moved by the duet. She grinned self-consciously and wiped a tear away. "You made me cry," she accused Roscoe. "You're too good. And we're not bad together, eh?"

"If you say so, ma'am," Roscoe said, looking at Vonda respectfully. He swallowed, his Adam's apple bobbing spectacularly.

Vonda turned to Mitch. "I want him on the first album I do for you. I want at least one duet with him. Probably two. In return, I'll do a song with him on his debut album. What do you say?"

Roscoe looked dazzled at the prospect. Mitch shrugged lazily. "If it sells records, I'm for it," he muttered casually. "Try a faster number, you two. Let's hear what you can do."

Vonda winked at Roscoe, which made him radiant. "He wants to see what we can do, Slim. Let's show him."

The two of them were off again, notes filling the air like an incredible brightness. For the first time, Dinah thought, she was truly beginning to appreciate this music, comprehend its claims on the emotions.

Well after midnight, Vonda handed the guitar back to Mitch. She stifled a yawn behind one bejeweled hand and laughed. "This has been wonderful. Just what the doctor ordered." She went suddenly silent. Her dark eyes met Mitch's cat-green ones. "I mean it's been wonderful," she finished softly. "Thanks."

"My pleasure," Mitch replied easily, but he scrutinized Vonda's beautiful face as if he could read things there that no one else could. He was suddenly solemn. "Are you all right?" he asked with concern. "It's late. You must be tired. Do you want to spend the night? I've got plenty of room. You don't have to go clear back."

Dinah sat still, pretending to be invisible. She felt somehow humiliated. She knew a courteous host could ask a late-staying guest to stay over. But she also knew that what existed between Mitch and Vonda was more complex than an ordinary business relationship, despite what Vonda had told her earlier.

Vonda shook her head, her fiery hair glistening. She glanced significantly at Roscoe and Dinah. "Not tonight," she said nervously. "You've already got company. I'll see you another time. Soon?"

Her voice seemed to hold a subtle plea. Mitch smiled. "Soon," he promised. "And for as long as you need me."

She turned and kissed Roscoe good-night, making him blush. "You're going to be a great star, honey," she assured him. "Trust me. I can see into the future."

Roscoe blushed harder and stuttered and shifted uncomfortably. Impulsively Vonda kissed him again, which completely robbed him of the power of speech.

Vonda thrust her hand out to Dinah, staring down at her with a strange expression in her long-lashed eyes. "Take good care of this boy, you hear?'' she stated. "This business—it's hard on a person. Stand watch over him.''

"I intend to,'' Dinah replied, confused.

"Take real good care of him,'' Vonda repeated. Something in her voice was almost ominous. Dinah looked at her in bewilderment.

Then Mitch escorted Vonda to her waiting chauffeur. Roscoe stared after her, awestruck. "I feel like I've done been to heaven,'' he said reverently.

Dinah shot him a look intended to snap him back to reality. It failed.

"I'd be hopeless in deep love with her,'' Roscoe continued raptly, "if only she wasn't so old.''

It was Dinah's turn to look stunned. "She's only thirty or so,'' she said.

Roscoe gave a shrug. "That don't seem old to you,'' he said innocently. "But if you was young, it would.''

That's it, Dinah thought with absolute fatality. My ego is gone. Destroyed. Everybody today has had a whack at it.

She was put further off balance when Mitch reentered, a large smear of Vonda's rosy lipstick on his cheek.

"Roscoe,'' Mitch said. "Your singing was inspired tonight. Miss Rainy lifted you to new heights.'' He poured himself a tumbler of bourbon. He ignored Dinah and concentrated on the boy. "Don't be overawed by her,'' he advised. "She won't like it. She wants people to feel comfortable around her. The two of you will probably be working together, so you may as well get used to her.''

"Yessir,'' Roscoe answered politely. "I just never met nobody famous before.'' It was clear the night had been magical for him.

"You should go to bed, Roscoe,'' Dinah urged. "You have to be at the dentist's at seven. It's the only time you could get in on such short notice.''

Roscoe grimaced slightly, but even the specter of his dentist's appointment didn't take the light from his face. He went upstairs without protest. To dream, doubtless, of a version of Vonda Rainy his own age.

"I hope he isn't getting a crush on her," Mitch murmured. "Vonda overpowers people sometimes. Without even meaning to. She walks into a room and men fall in love with her. Including ones far more sensible than Roscoe."

Including you? Dinah thought pessimistically. But she merely shrugged coolly. "Roscoe thinks we're all over the hill. I think he's wondering what she was like at sweet sixteen."

"Much as she is now, I suppose," he mused, examining the play of light on the ice cubes in his glass. "Gorgeous. Talented. Driven. Full of emotion. It's the emotion that lets her sing the way she does. I saw the way their first song hit you. If they can even make you feel, of all people, I'll sell millions of records. Maybe trillions." He downed his drink.

His voice had an unexpected edge. Her shoulders stiffened at the gibe. "I think I'll go to bed myself," she said with as much dignity as she could muster.

She started toward the stairs, but agilely he blocked her path. "What were you like at sweet sixteen?" he asked, the old taunt in his voice. "Did you love him then, this wonderful fiancé of yours? Is that why the song touched you? It made you think of him?"

He set his glass on a nearby table and attempted to take Dinah's hand in his. She drew back, eluding him. "At sixteen I was the same Goody Two Shoes I am now." She bit off the words. "Possibly even more boring, if you can imagine that."

"I don't find you boring," he answered, his voice suggestively low.

She looked up at him. With his widow's peak and angular brows, he looked as if he were born to mock. Her heart beat swiftly, her breath seemed trapped in her chest. She felt peculiar all over. But, she reminded herself sharply, less than ten minutes ago, he had given Vonda that intimate look and asked her to spend the night. The rosy smear of her lipstick was still on his cheek.

"I did think of... of Dennis when they sang," she said rebelliously. She couldn't bear to let Mitch see how tangled her emotions were. "We were together when we were sixteen. We've been together forever—"

Suddenly the burden of her conflicting emotions became too much. For the second time that night tears filled her sapphire eyes.

She had thought of Dennis, but only of all the things he had never made her feel—including love. They had been together for years because other people had thought they should be together, and they had been too naive or too cowardly to rebel.

Now she had found Mitch Carey, a man to whom she was so strongly drawn that it nearly paralyzed her with fear and longing. He could almost stop her heart by looking at her. But the beautiful Vonda Rainy had claims on him.

An immense and dark chasm seemed to yawn at her feet. She was engaged to a man she didn't love. She wanted a man she shouldn't have who was involved with a woman far more beautiful and intriguing than she.

"What's the matter with you?" Mitch demanded, staring stony-faced at the tears that gleamed in her eyes.

"Nothing," she returned sharply. She kept looking at the floor. Ashamed of her tears, she brushed her hand across her eyes, but new ones rose immediately.

Almost roughly Mitch put his hand beneath her chin and raised her face to his. He studied her with dispassion, but something cold glittered in his eyes. The look frightened her and made her want him at the same time. He would never be weak or indecisive, wondering what to do next. He would always know. And be stronger than she.

"My God," he said slowly, poring over her face. "You really love him that much? And miss him?"

Dinah's heart wrenched. She was too ashamed to admit that the feelings she had for Dennis were nothing compared to the emotions Mitch stirred within her. And so she lied.

"Yes," she said tightly. "He and I are alike—the same kind. I miss him. I wish I were anywhere but here." In truth she didn't miss Dennis at all, only the comfort of her lost illusions.

"So that's the way it is," he said between clenched teeth. He stretched out his arm as if he would place his hand against the curve of her cheek. Then he checked himself. A vein jumped in his temple and deliberately he drew his hand back. "You and he are alike. Old families. Old money. The American aristocrats. I suppose I should be intimidated. I'm not. Maybe that's my problem."

"Maybe it is," Dinah said tartly, regretting her words immediately. She saw him stiffen. She knew she had said the wrong thing.

This time he reached for her without hesitation. His hand gripped her small, stubborn jaw and forced her to keep her face turned up to his. His expressive mouth was coldly furious. "I wish I were somewhere else myself," he said with an icy smile. "With someone else. A woman whose blood was more red than blue. One not quite so civilized. And certainly one not quite so committed to making the mistake of her life."

"What mistake?" she asked miserably.

He bent his face nearer to hers, one eyebrow lifted cynically. His fingers seemed to burn into her skin. "The mistake of going back to Connecticut," he rasped. "Of marrying this childhood sweetheart so the two of you can go on being childish and sweet and insulated from reality. And mostly, the mistake of never once in your life having admitted to any emotion that wasn't tame, decorous, proper, prescribed and in accord with the stiff-necked MacNeil code. Lord, what a waste. What a bloody terrible waste."

She stood quite still, the way an endangered deer freezes in its tracks. She had the panicky feeling that if he kissed her, she would give herself to him, and her life would be unalterably changed.

He shook his head, releasing her. He stepped to the bar, poured himself another shot of bourbon. He tossed her a sardonic look. "What will you do when you get back to Connecticut?" he asked, his lip curling. "Besides marry the boy wonder? I suppose he is a boy wonder, eh? Lots of venerable ancestors and a charmed future with lots of venerable money."

Dinah ignored what he said about Dennis. She raised her chin defiantly. "I'm going to Yale," she said. "I'll get my master's degree. I'll work in the MacNeil Museum in New Haven." It suddenly sounded like an extraordinarily dreary existence, but she kept her head high.

"Ah," he said sarcastically. "How exciting. The MacNeil Museum. I've been there. Shrine to the history of steel, isn't it? Stimulating subject. One a woman might be proud to dedicate her life to. Indeed, perhaps the perfect choice for you. You with so much steel in your spine."

Dinah's spine felt anything but steely. Still, she held herself as tall as possible. "Are you quite done?" she asked. "I'd like to go to bed now."

"So would I," he stated. "Only, being merely human, I wouldn't like to go alone."

"Then," Dinah replied primly, starting up the stairs, "it's too bad Miss Rainy didn't stay, isn't it?"

In a flash he was at her side. His brows were raised, his expression wry. "You don't often take a cheap shot. When you do, though, it's very cheap indeed. Vonda and I—"

Icily, Dinah stepped back, knowing she had to avoid his touch. "You don't understand," she said sweetly. "I don't care anything about Vonda and you. I don't want to hear anything about Vonda and you. All I want to do is finish my job and get out of here."

"Even if Roscoe might need more than three lousy weeks out of your upper-class little life?" he jeered. "Wake up and smell the coffee, lady. Can't you tell how dangerous this business is? If anybody knows, it's me. If you don't believe me, ask Vonda. We've both seen what it can do to a person. Can't you understand how much this boy is going to need somebody to help him?"

"Why me?" cried Dinah in sudden passion. It was the question that had haunted her from the beginning. "Why me?" She repeated the words so vehemently that his eyes narrowed in surprise. "You want him for your own profit, you watch out for him. Or let Vonda do it. She discovered him. She's responsible for all this."

"Neither Vonda nor I have the time," he shot back. "We already have full-time careers."

"So do I," she retorted, but she knew it was a lie. Frustrated, she started to flee up the stairs carefully holding her full black skirt into modest place. But her feelings were running high, and for once she let them run. She looked over her shoulder and caught Mitch watching her with amused cynicism.

"Why is it always me that's supposed to be looking after Roscoe?" she asked, her eyes flashing. "Why do you always say it's my duty? As if I'm the only person who can rescue him from some horrible fate?''

She stopped at the landing and stared down at Mitch. She gripped the banister and wished the enormous diamond weren't twinkling on her hand. ''Why?'' she demanded again. ''Why am I the only chance he's got?''

He leaned against the wall. He looked up at her calmly. Rudely, he yawned. ''Maybe you've got it backward.'' He smiled. ''Maybe he's the only chance you've got. Before you become a museum piece in New Haven. I've always thought of museums as cluttered, dusty old places. Yours doesn't have ... mice, by any chance, does it?''

''Oh!'' she gasped in utter frustration. She ran the rest of the way up the stairs, not bothering to keep her skirt in place.

Mitch watched after her, one eyebrow cocked. He caught a stimulating glimpse of swiftly moving white knees, an all too brief flash of pale and slender thigh.

He heard her door slam with unladylike force. He raised his glass toward the stairs. ''Good night, dear Miss Mac-Neil,'' he said softly. ''Sweet, virginal, aristocratic and mouseless dreams.''

He drained his bourbon and swore softly to himself.

DINAH SAT on the edge of the bed, breathing hard. She tried to think over her day in objective and orderly fashion. She could not. Her mind was a jumble of shocks. She didn't love Dennis. Dennis didn't love her. She loved Mitch Carey. So, probably, did Vonda Rainy. And Mitch loved—whom? What? Perhaps he loved nothing but power. Perhaps he needed it the way other men needed air. He wanted power over her for no other reason than that she was there.

She wanted to run. She wanted to leave Nashville because it had upset her whole idea of what was real and what was not. Suddenly she knew she couldn't go back to Connecticut and work in the steel museum if her life depended on it.

She glanced at her hands and found she was twisting her ring again, as if it were a shackle she perpetually tried to escape. This couldn't go on, she thought desperately. If nothing else, she had to take off Dennis's ring before it drove her mad. She would tell Dennis now.

Without thinking she picked up the rhinestone-studded telephone and dialed his number. There was a ring, a click, a buzz, and then the tinny voice of Dennis's answering machine.

"Hello, hello, hello. This is Dennis Lingle. Tonight I've been invited to a reception at the home of Miss Twissle, the retiring professor of harp, clavichord and harmonium. Please leave your name, number and message and I'll call you at my first convenience tomorrow. Have a pleasant evening!"

Dinah listened to the message, the horror of realization dawning. Of course Dennis wouldn't be answering his phone. She was tempted to leave a message telling him where he could take his harp, his reception and himself. Breeding triumphed, however. She set down the receiver without leaving any message at all. She felt empty, trapped and defeated.

She had no idea who she would get to look after Roscoe after she'd gone. Mitch was right—she should stay with the boy. But she couldn't. For the sake of her own sanity, she simply could not. She would have to escape from everything: Connecticut and Dennis; Nashville and Roscoe and her conscience; and most of all from Mitch Carey.

CHAPTER EIGHT

ROSCOE WAS NO LONGER bewitched by Nashville when Dinah steered him out of the dentist's office. His jaw was full of Novocain and his mind was full of dread—he had two more appointments the next two days. He might already have the voice of a star, but his teeth were going to take work. She took him home and sent him to bed.

She went back to her room, squared her shoulders and sat down to call Dennis. In all her confusion, one thing was clear. She couldn't continue to wear his ring. She must be the one to say what they both knew.

But when she dialed his number, all she got was the answering machine.

"Hello, hello, hello! This is Dennis Lingle. Tonight I've been invited to a reception at the home of Miss Twissle, the retiring professor of harp, clavichord and harmonium..."

Dinah frowned and rechecked her watch. The message was the same as the previous night's. How unlike Dennis not to have erased it and changed it after breakfast. Again she hung up the phone without leaving a message. She could hardly say, "Please call. I want to break our engagement." She was too upset to think of a tactful alternative.

Instead, she checked on Roscoe, then drove back into downtown Nashville. It was finally time for her audience with the agent.

THE AGENT, Stephen Fleetwood, was a high-strung man who had bags under his eyes and smoked endlessly. "I'll take this kid on," he said in his gravelly voice, his pale face harsh. "But only because he's Mitch Carey's protégé. I have a hunch that Carey is going to do something big in this town. He's not flighty like his brother. This guy's got smarts. He's tight-mouthed about his past, but somehow he knows the recording business. It's like it's in his blood."

"I know he's intelligent," Dinah said, anxious for help. "But can I trust him?"

"In this business I wouldn't trust my own mother," Fleetwood answered shortly. "But miracles happen. It's possible." With restless hands, he lit another cigarette.

"Who is he, really?" she asked in near desperation. "He and his brother—how did they end up in Nashville? What did they do before?"

Fleetwood shrugged. "Who knows?" He peered at her through blue coils of smoke. "Bobby Carey was a plunger— the type that throws himself headlong into things. He was an easy mark for a fast talker like Lucky Bucky. He was also a lush."

"A lush?" Dinah's smooth brow furrowed. "You mean he drank?"

"Precisely," Fleetwood concurred without sympathy. "But one thing he didn't do was talk about his past. Neither does Mitch Carey. Nobody knows anything about them. Except rumors. In this business there's always the rumors."

"What...what sort of rumors?" Dinah asked, feeling immoral for asking about gossip. She almost succeeded in convincing herself she had a right to know—for Roscoe's sake.

Fleetwood sighed derisively. "Every sort. The most persistent is that he was a vice president of Mecca Records. That he has important connections."

"Mecca Records?" Dinah asked, taken aback. Mecca was one of the biggest record companies in the country. It made sense. Experience with Mecca would give him the confidence to take on Diamond Horseshoe.

"That's one story," Fleetwood said, obviously displeased with its validity. "Another is that he and Bobby are the illegitimate sons of a rich recluse who made a fortune in movies and aviation. Another is that they come from a wealthy family, but the wealth wasn't earned with—shall we say—complete honesty. Another is he's been in the record business in Germany. And, finally, there's one that music was always a passion with both brothers, but the family didn't approve."

"I wonder if any of that's true," Dinah stated, bewildered.

He shrugged again with utter cynicism. "Who knows? Who cares? The important thing is whether he knows his stuff. I think he does. That's why I'm willing to take on your boy, sight unseen. Carey's got me interested."

Dinah studied the tense, hard-faced man before her. "Why?" she almost begged. "Why does he have you interested?"

"Maybe because I hear he's got some unexpected talent lined up. Your boy, for instance. A woman from Canada, for instance. A group from Arkansas, for instance. Maybe because I hear he's going to develop and keep this talent by a novel method—by treating it right. Or maybe because he's been the only man in Nashville smart enough to tempt Vonda Rainy away from the people who've been controlling her."

"Oh," Dinah said tonelessly. It had come down to Vonda Rainy again.

Fleetwood crushed out his cigarette and lit another. "Everybody in town knows he wants her," he wheezed. "She wants more freedom, and he's the only man in town brave enough to break the formula and give it to her. They want and need each other. As for your boy, Roscoe—he's pure and basic country—unspoiled. That's an important trend at present. Back to basics."

Dinah tried to ignore the lash of pain Fleetwood's simple words had inflicted: *"They want and need each other."* She felt somehow stricken.

"My guess," Fleetwood said cannily, "is Carey will use Vonda to bring in the fast money for the company. But he'll use the boy to build on, to make money in the long run. A lot of money, a gold mine, in fact. If he's right about the kid—then I want a piece of the action."

Dinah weighed this information. She shifted uncomfortably. If Roscoe had such potential, her responsibility to him seemed heavier than ever. She sat in silence. Stephen Fleetwood studied her with an eye as pitiless as that of a bird of prey. She twisted her ring. He watched the movement with interest. Almost against her will, she twisted the ring again, as if it hurt her.

"I sense there's one more question you want to ask," he rasped at last. "You want to ask about Carey and Vonda Rainy. To know if their relationship is just business."

Embarrassed, Dinah met his glittering gaze. Was she that transparent?

She decided to brazen it out. "Well, is it?" she asked, her chin high in her shamelessness. "Strictly business between them, that is?"

"You seem like a nice girl," said Stephen Fleetwood. He glanced at her ring. "All I hear is rumors. Understand that.

But the smart money says no, it isn't strictly business. Another rumor is he's not afraid to use any woman who can help him get what he wants. Understand that, also. For instance, I hear he used you to get Lucky Bucky to walk out— a very cagey move. Anybody's who's ever fired the guy has ended up in an endless lawsuit. You wonder why I'm telling you this? The word is out that your family is important. I wouldn't want them to think I was less than frank with you. This much isn't rumor. You're just a kid yourself. He's a man of the world."

Dinah sat straight, but she felt slightly numbed with shock. Fleetwood stared at her unblinkingly through the smoke. "You understand?" he queried, his face as hard as before.

He was warning her only out of deference to her family's power. Perhaps that was the only reason he had troubled to give her any information at all. But he had warned her, nevertheless. She nodded. "I understand," she said stiffly. "Thank you."

"Think nothing of it," he said. "Your family might own some record stock someday."

Not if I can help it, Dinah thought bitterly. She wanted to stay as far from this deceptive, complex and illusory business as possible.

IT WAS ALMOST NOON when she left Fleetwood's office, so she wandered down Division Street until she came to an uncrowded restaurant. She had to eat, she told herself, even if she didn't feel like it.

Neither her family nor Dennis realized that she constantly pushed herself to the limits of her strength. She had fooled them into thinking she had at last developed the traditional iron constitution of the MacNeils. Only Mitch had sensed the truth and sensed it immediately.

She sat back in a black leatherette booth and studied the menu without interest. Her head ached. There was so much to be done for Roscoe and no one but her to do it.

She ordered a salad, then sat worrying about Roscoe and musing over which rumor of Mitch's past might be true. She wondered, in a rare burst of superstition, if Mitch had simply appeared in Nashville out of thin air, smiling his devilish smile and trailing a faint whiff of brimstone.

Dinah spent the rest of the afternoon at the library, poring over books about Nashville and the music industry. Mitch was not yet home when she arrived at the mansion, and Roscoe was in the music room, holding an ice pack to his jaw. He said he never wanted to see another dentist as long as he lived. She told him firmly he would be seeing the same one tomorrow—and the next day. He groaned and sank back into the sofa cushions, too morose to talk.

Once in her room she tried to call Dennis again, but got only his answering machine again. The message was new. "Cheery day! This is Dennis Lingle. I'm having supper with some chums from the string section. Then I'm going to an oboe recital—busy, busy, busy! Please leave your name, number and business, and I'll call you tomorrow, as soon as possible. Have a nice evening! Ta!"

Dinah listened to the beep that signaled the answering machine was ready to record her message. She wanted to cry out, "Dennis, where are you? We have to talk! We have to!"

Instead she hung up without saying anything. Surely Dennis would call her soon.

Yet part of her was always grateful that Dennis hadn't answered. If she did break the engagement, then she could take off the ring. And if she took off the ring, she would feel naked when she saw Mitch again. Mitch was not offering her the safety of an engagement. He offered nothing but danger.

She tried to call Dennis again at seven, and at eight, just before Mitch arrived. All she got was the maddening recording. Then Mitch knocked at her door and took her down to the patio for supper. Her heart hammered when she saw him, hammered still harder when she realized that only the two of them would be dining. Roscoe, Mitch explained wryly, was still in dental recovery.

Why, thought Dinah distractedly, did the man have to sound so sexy even when he was talking about somebody else's bicuspids? He pulled out a chair for her, and his arm accidentally brushed her bare one. Her nerves sang out like too-taut strings. He didn't seem affected in the least.

"Did you have a good day?" Dinah asked, as they sat in the warm dusk, sipping white wine. Her question sounded inane and stilted to her.

He raised an eyebrow and regarded her with mock patience. "Spoken with all the sincerity of a parrot. Yes, thank you. And how was your day? Your visit to the agent? And your lunch? You should've eaten more than a salad, by the way. Have a nice trip to the library?"

Dinah set down her glass and glared at him in disbelief. "How do you know all that? Do you have someone spying on me?"

He took an olive and ate it with a gourmet's thoughtfulness. "I get around," he said vaguely. "Besides, I have a responsibility to keep an eye on you. You're the new girl in town. The babe in the woods."

"I'm no babe," she stated with spirit. "And this is no mere woods. It's a jungle out there."

"Tsk," he warned, reaching for another olive. "Please don't descend to clichés. You're too bright."

"I spent the afternoon reading about this business," she said darkly. "It seems to me that too many stars have paid too high a price for success."

"The failures have paid too high a price for failure, too," he replied. "Believe me, I know. I've been telling you this is a dangerous business, especially for somebody as young and impressionable as Roscoe. He's going to need an immense amount of guidance. But it took books to finally make it clear to you. That's how you like to learn, isn't it? From books? Not from life."

"You have no idea at all how or what I learn," she parried. "None."

"Wrong," he answered with assurance. "The very fact you went to the library shows I'm right. Nashville throbs around you, live and electric and real—and how do you try to find out about it? From books. Typical, Dinah. You trust the printed word more than the world at your doorstep. But I'll reach you however I can. I have a book for you myself. One on Hank Williams—Roscoe's idol."

"I don't want to read it," she said rebelliously. "I'm sure he was a genius and that all sorts of terrible things happened to him and he ended up dead at thirty, like some brilliant, misguided poet."

"Actually," Mitch mused, "he was dead at twenty-nine. He couldn't handle fame. Nobody was there who could help him. And the world hasn't seen his kind of talent again, until maybe now—our skinny friend with the ice pack in there."

She stared at the enigmatic dark-haired man across from her. The candlelight made shadows dance over his sculpted features. "You really believe he's that good?" she asked almost fearfully.

"I know he's that good," Mitch replied. "And a few people in town, the really smart ones, are beginning to suspect."

"Like Stephen Fleetwood—the agent," she murmured unhappily.

He picked up his wineglass and looked at her ironically over its rim. "Precisely. Fleetwood's a cynical motor-mouth, but he'll keep a very good watch over Roscoe's contracts. As for Roscoe's soul—which is what you claim to be interested in helping him keep—well, there's nobody around to watch out for that, but you."

She put down her fork. The meal was delightful, roast Cornish hens stuffed with wild rice and mushrooms, but once more she had lost her appetite. "I'm just starting to understand the pressure he's going to face," she murmured unhappily. "The touring, the endless road trips, crazy hours, the temptation to take a pill to go to sleep and then another one to wake up and then another one to keep going. The pressure to match the last success or come back from a failure. The people who'll cheat you and the people who'll toady to you. But what I don't understand is why anyone thinks I can guide Roscoe through this morass. It's as new to me as it is to him."

Mitch finished his wine and poured more. "It should be obvious, my dear Miss MacNeil. It's because you're incorruptible."

"Incorruptible?" Dinah questioned, her eyes widening. "What do you mean?"

"Just what I say. You'll never be bought. Furthermore, you have the one indefinable thing that can't be bought, but could be passed on to someone who needs it. Someone like Roscoe, for instance."

"What's that?" she asked suspiciously.

"Class," he said with a smile. "Quality. Grace. Confidence. And, of course, those manners that are so dear to you."

The candlelight seemed to dance in his eyes, making her feel slightly intoxicated. "If I'm all that worthy," she said with a false sophistication, "I should also be able to see through flattery. And I do." She raised her glass to him. "Nice try, Mr. Carey. But not good enough. You somehow used me to get rid of Lucky Bucky. I don't plan to stick around to be used again."

"All's fair in love, war and getting rid of Lucky Bucky," he returned. "And I don't flatter. Flattery is praise that's excessive or insincere. My remarks were neither. I don't think you're without flaw. There's always the matter of your insistence on marrying that cold fish in Connecticut. And then hiding yourself away in a steel museum."

"You're terribly eager to criticize my life," Dinah replied defensively. "But I notice you never say much about your own. I've been in this town long enough to hear rumors about you. I'd like to know the truth."

"Do you care?" he asked with taunting insolence.

"Only for Roscoe's sake," she answered, feeling her cheeks start to burn. "I, personally, could not care less."

"Then you, personally, don't need to know," he retorted, his smile falling away. "I have my reasons for keeping my past quiet. Sound business reasons."

"Do you have reasons for keeping your real relationship with Miss Rainy quiet, too?" she challenged.

He studied her features for an intimidating moment. The candlelight played, making shadows shift over his face. "Do you care?" he asked again quietly.

She was not about to reveal she cared so much that she ached. "Of course I don't care," she said coolly. "I'm simply curious."

"I have certain loyalties to Vonda," he returned, even more coolly. "And reasons for keeping quiet about her personal life. Reasons I would expect a lady such as yourself to understand."

"Of course," she said in her most civilized tone.

"All these matters are unimportant, anyway," he commented, as if suddenly bored by the conversation. "Let's discuss something important. Like going dancing tonight."

She set down her glass and looked at him helplessly. He was a maddening man, who always set her head spinning until she was totally disoriented. He had practically admitted his affair with Vonda, yet now he was asking her out. "Dancing?" she asked in disbelief. "You don't mean country dancing, do you? Because I haven't the faintest idea how."

"It's easy," he said, reaching across the table and refilling her glass. "The Texas Two-Step is a classic Western dance. It's ridiculously easy. I simply put my arms around you. And then I push you around."

Dinah glowered at him. "I think," she said with asperity, "that you've done too much of that already."

"Putting my arms around you?" he asked suggestively. "Wrong. I haven't done nearly enough."

"No," she countered. "Pushing me around. You've done altogether too much of it, and I don't need any more."

He shrugged carelessly. "Pushing you around is, I'll admit, an inelegant way to describe it. All right, I lead or I guide you—whatever. You'll like it. I promise."

"No," she argued, making herself spear another forkful of food. "If you want to go dancing, take someone else. I'm sure there are legions of women who'd be delighted."

He made an unsuccessful attempt to look modest. "Oh, maybe not legions."

"I'm staying here," she said with finality, though her heart drummed treacherously. "I'm expecting a phone call."

His face, mocking a moment before, darkened. "Oh," he said tonelessly. "From your peerless fiancé, no doubt. You've assured me how mature and adjusted he is. He won't mind if I take you out to experience a bit of native Nashville culture."

Dinah set down her fork again in frustration. Mitch was toying with her. Perhaps he didn't even realize how cruelly his games hurt. She would have danced with him anywhere, to any music, simply to be in his arms. But she couldn't. "No," she replied. "He wouldn't mind. But I mind. I want to talk to him."

"Ah. Still sticking with your own kind," he said curtly. "I hope you have a fascinating conversation. He must be a marvelous fellow. His manners, undoubtedly. And his perfect breeding." He rose from the table and tossed down his napkin. "I'll find someone else who's not above a little honky-tonking. Unlike your boyfriend, I'd rather have my hands on a warm, live woman than a cold phone. You don't mind if I leave you here, I take it."

"Of course not," Dinah said primly, holding her head high.

He started to leave, but paused behind her chair. She could feel his presence, and the silence between them seemed to vibrate, to strike her in palpable waves.

Slowly he bent and pressed his lips against the back of her neck. Although his mouth was hot against her smooth flesh, shivers of cold ran through her, shocking and tingling her.

"Delicious," he said softly. "Like all forbidden fruit." His breath warmly tickled her nape. "I'll see you. In the meantime, keep eating. Even an ice princess needs food,

Dinah. Your impeccable pedigree doesn't mean you're so refined that you can live on air.''

Then he was gone.

Dinah sat in the falling darkness, her heart torn with confusion. She picked at her food, trying to eat, like the obedient and dutiful person she had always been.

When the bearded servant came and told her there was a long-distance phone call for her, she walked as slowly as possible to her room to take it. She was about to tell Dennis goodbye. And she would be saying goodbye, as well, to herself, the self she had always known and thought she understood.

CHAPTER NINE

"DINAH!" Dennis said in true shock. "Break our engagement? What do you mean? Where's the cool-headed sensible Dinah I've always known?"

Good question, Dinah thought with dark humor. Where had that young woman gone? She had started to disappear slowly in Kakexia; in Nashville she seemed to have vanished completely.

"This is altogether too rash," Dennis said confidently. "It's not reasoned out. Have you thought of how this will affect our families? How disappointed your mother will be? To say nothing of my mother! They'll both be devastated. You must take time to think."

"I have thought," she countered. "In the back of my mind I've been thinking about it a long time. For instance, you didn't really care when I went to Kakexia, did you? You let me go off without a single regret—and never came to see me once. I think you were relieved that I was far away."

"That's not fair," Dennis sniffed. "It's part of your family tradition that you go off to Kakexia or some awful place for a year—"

"Kakexia was not an awful place," Dinah returned with spirit. "It has many fine, upstanding, courageous people—"

"And not a symphony orchestra within miles, just that wretched country music," he rebuked her. "You had your duties. I had mine. Really, Dinah, I'm surprised. You sound petty, almost jealous. It was out of my very respect for you that I let you follow your interests."

"Was it out of respect you let me come to Nashville?" Dinah demanded.

"Certainly," Dennis said piously. "I told you that I wouldn't quash your personhood—"

"Dennis," Dinah said, her voice dangerously even, "will you please stop using that dreadful word."

"What dreadful word?" he demanded in surprise.

"Personhood," Dinah countered. "It sounds so...trendy. And when I try to discuss the difficulties I'm having here, you chatter about not having negative thoughts and tell me not to worry about coming home. You don't sound like a man in love. You sound like a man who's glad I'm gone."

There was a moment of ominous silence. "Dinah," he said at last, "I thought you wanted to stay and help little Rufus. I thought you considered it your responsibility. Forgive me if I offended you."

"His name is Roscoe, not Rufus," Dinah told him emphatically. "Yes, I want to help him, but no, I don't want to stay in Nashville until—until he's twenty-one or something, for heaven's sake! I don't even know if I'm the right person to help him!"

"Then it's most certainly your duty to stay there until you find the person who is right, isn't it?" Dennis asked sweetly. "I know you, Dinah. Your conscience would never let you walk off and leave the child. You have to stay until you find someone to take over for you. It's not like you to get so upset over such clear-cut moral choices. You're overwrought."

"I'm not just overwrought," Dinah muttered grimly. "I'm overwhelmed. There's nothing clear-cut here. Everything's as confusing as possible. And you, Dennis, are evading the issue. You don't love me, do you?"

Another uncomfortable silence followed. "Dinah," Dennis said at last, "has something happened that makes you think you don't love me? I mean, you've loved me since we were eleven. Don't you remember? You had a sinus infection, and Mother sent me over to your house to read you *Alice's Adventures in Wonderland* and play piano for you. We had a lovely time, even if you did snuffle so alarmingly. You told me afterward that you'd never had so much fun when you'd had a cold before."

"Dennis, I've been fond of you for years, but perhaps we've been confusing fondness with love. We're more like brother and sister than . . . than lovers."

"Lovers! Dinah! Please!" Dennis cried with horror. "What's happened to you? Is it this . . . this man you mentioned? The one in Nashville?"

"Yes," Dinah said simply. She realized that for the first time in years she was being frank with Dennis. It was a heady feeling, intoxicating almost.

"This man—has he expressed deep feelings for you, as well?" Dennis asked in the same appalled tone.

"No," Dinah said frankly. "No deep feelings at all. I'm nothing to him. Just another woman. One of many."

"Dinah, you're making a terrible mistake," Dennis said fretfully. "You can't break our engagement over a man who doesn't even care for you. Oh, dear, you've always been so naive. You've never understood how the world works."

"Dennis, I don't want to be your enemy," Dinah stated earnestly, "but our engagement has been a farce and our marriage would be a disaster. I can't wear your ring any longer. I just can't. Please understand."

"Dinah," he said, more stern than she'd ever heard him, "if that's how you feel, I'll honor your wishes. But on one condition. Think this over first. If you feel the same in four weeks, then we'll break the engagement. But until then, out of regard for the affection we've shared, and out of respect for our families, please wear the ring. And keep this conversation confidential—between us only. For I must say, my feelings are more confused than I can tell you. I'm highly disturbed. I need time to cope."

Dennis did sound uncharacteristically unhappy. She swallowed hard. Four weeks. She supposed she owed him that. She would continue the charade for four more weeks. By then, perhaps, she would have found someone to look after Roscoe, and she would be back in Connecticut, to break the engagement in the proper way. She swallowed again.

"Dinah," wheedled Dennis, "surely you are civilized enough, generous enough, honorable enough to give me four weeks. Otherwise I don't know how I'll ever begin to explain to Mother...or for that matter to your mother— who'll be even more upset—laid low, in fact. You know how fond your mother and I are of each other."

"Don't worry," she said at last, defeat in her voice. "You're probably right. This seems sudden. Although it really isn't, and I think you know it as well as I do. Four more weeks? Certainly. And I won't say anything to anyone."

"Bless you, Dinah," he said gently. "Oh, dear, I'm afraid the recital is starting up again—I must go. Perhaps music will soothe me. This has been a most upsetting conversation, Dinah. I—I can't tell you how it's affected me."

When Dinah hung up, she felt unhappy and guilty. Dennis hadn't reacted like a man deeply in love. And yet he had been truly dismayed. Maybe in his own shallow, burbling way, he cared for her. But she had stopped caring for him. Because of a dark-haired man with wicked green eyes. A man like Mitch Carey would only want her for a short time—until he'd proved to himself he could have her. Perhaps only a tame and predictable man like Dennis could care for her at all. But that was no longer enough.

She looked at her huge and meaningless engagement ring. It was no doubt best to keep wearing it. It was the only thing shielding her from Mitch Carey's seductive powers—and her own foolish yearning for him.

Her room seemed more of a prison than ever. She wandered downstairs to join Roscoe. But he wasn't there, the maid informed her. He had taken his ice pack and gone to bed to have nightmares about drills and dental picks. Dinah sighed sympathetically and strolled out into the big sun room with its choking tangle of tropical plants.

There was so much to teach Roscoe, she mused. And somehow, for his own good, she should convince him to go on with his education. But how could she ever succeed with Nashville offering so many sparkling temptations? But without more schooling, he was going to be ever at the mercy of those more knowledgeable than he. In short, he would always be a potential victim. The best thing she could do was to teach him to take care of himself. But how— against such odds? And with so little time?

Her brooding was interrupted by the maid. "I thought you were out here, Miss MacNeil," the girl said. "I know it's late, but Mr. Williston would like to see you."

Dinah looked at the girl in puzzlement. "Mr. Williston?" she asked. "He must want Mr. Carey. And Mr. Carey's out."

"No, ma'am," the maid said, tucking an errant lock back into her wilting beehive hairdo. "He says it's you he wants to see. Should I show him in?"

Why not, Dinah's dazed mind asked. "Certainly," she said without conviction. She didn't see how Lucky Bucky could make the evening any worse than it was. "I'll see him here," she added. What better place, she thought ironically, than this facsimile of a jungle.

Lucky Bucky entered shortly, dressed in white, as if he were some bloated parody of a white knight. He held a snowy Stetson in his pudgy hands. Its band was made of gray-and-white python skin and matched his expensive boots.

She turned to him. In spite of her smallness, she managed to impart a truly regal quality to her motion. "I don't know what business you have with me, Mr. Williston," she said evenly. "Mr. Carey is your employer—and he's not here."

"I know he ain't," Lucky Bucky said, nervously fingering his hat. "He's down at a club called the Natchez Trace. With Vonda Rainy. I figured you was here."

"Oh." Dinah's heart tightened at the news. She pretended to be interested in a large white orchid. "And what do you think I can do for you, Mr. Williston?"

He stood for a few seconds in awkward silence, playing with his hat. "Forgive me, ma'am," he said at last.

She looked up at him in surprise. His face was red and he stared at the tiled floor. He pushed a fallen flower petal with the toe of his boot.

"Forgive you?" she asked in genuine surprise.

"Yes'm," he muttered, still not meeting her eyes. "I was mighty rude to you—and to the young man. I don't expect to handle Roscoe's promotion material. I know Mr. Carey wouldn't allow it, now that I went and said what I said and walked out the way I did. I reckon I just fell into his trap. He's a lot smarter than me, Mr. Carey is. A lot smarter than 'most everybody, ma'am. But I did want to say I was sorry."

Dinah studied him suspiciously. The big man, surrounded by thick vines and hothouse flowers, seemed both incongruous and insincere. "What do you mean, you 'fell into his trap'?"

He shrugged unhappily, like a man admitting his own stupidity. "He likes to set people against each other." Bucky sighed, still staring at the floor. "Let them do his dirty work for him. I got a contract with Diamond Horseshoe from Mr. Carey's brother, Bobby. Only Mr. Carey don't want to honor it. So he's tryin' to make me cut my own throat. And so far I've done a pretty good job of it."

"I don't understand," Dinah said cautiously, but she remembered Mitch's words in the office yesterday—how it was better that she anger Bucky than he do it himself. Stephen Fleetwood had said the same thing.

Bucky flushed more deeply, but he raised his head and his little blue eyes met her wide, questioning ones. "He had me scared to death of you before you even got here," Bucky said miserably. "Said who you was and how important you was and how I'd never be able to please such a high-class person. He said no matter what, though, I shouldn't let you push me around. And the next thing I know, I'm in such a state, I'm sayin' things I ought not and tellin' you I won't work with you. I didn't realize he was settin' us against each other on purpose."

"On purpose?" she asked. "What does he have to gain by setting us against each other?"

"He don't want to honor his contract to me," Bucky said, his lower lip thrust out. "He just ain't honest enough to fire me. Wants to force me to quit so I lose money. To say nothin' of losin' face. He enjoys seein' people lose face, he does. I ain't been around him long, but I been around him enough to know that."

Dinah held his unwavering gaze.

"He's played me against Vonda, too," Bucky said bitterly. "I worked with her before. We got along fine. Now, since Mr. Carey's here, stirring up trouble, she's turned against me, too.'' He sighed and looked in embarrassment out the big windows into the night. "I wouldn't mind, ma'am, if he told me he just didn't like my work. That'd be honest, and the world's got room for all kinds of opinions. What I mind is the way he uses us all against each other, so nobody can trust nobody.''

"Would you care to explain that remark?'' Dinah asked, although Bucky's words made a terrible sort of sense to her.

He shrugged again. "You against me. Vonda against me. You and Vonda against each other. Soon it'll be Vonda against the kid. You'll see—he'll keep everybody off balance by puttin' them against each other. That's his game, and he's good at it."

"What?'' she asked, nervously fingering the jagged leaves of an ivy. "Vonda and I against each other? Vonda and Roscoe against each other?''

"He'll try to make Vonda and Roscoe each think the other is a back stabber. He'll make them both so insecure they'll do anything Mitch Carey wants. As for you and Vonda, ma'am, that's pretty clear.''

"Unfortunately not to me, Mr. Williston,'' Dinah said, hoping she sounded calmer than she felt. "Vonda Rainy and I aren't set against each other. Nor can I see any possible gain for Mr. Carey if we were.''

Bucky's gaze brightened with malice. "Can't you, ma'am? He'll keep stringin' you along as long as it suits him—'cause he knows it's the key to gettin' the kid and 'cause it makes Vonda jealous. Mighty jealous. I've seen the gleam in his eyes when he looks at you. I see by the look on your face that he's got to you. He does that fast, he does— get to women. You be careful, ma'am. He'll use you every which way he can.''

"He wouldn't dare," she said with such vehemence that she accidentally pulled off a sprig of the ivy.

"He'd dare anything, ma'am," Bucky assured her. "That's why he scares me. Only man in my life who ever scared me. He don't care who he hurts. He's about to launch a company. He'll do anything. Don't let him fool you. He'll marry Vonda. She's desperate to get married again. To have kids before it's too late. And that's what he's offered her, ma'am. You think she'd sign up with this piddlin' little company for any other reason? But he won't ever want her to feel too sure of herself. Girl like yourself, young, educated, high class—well, you're bound to keep her off balance."

Bucky looked down at the floor again, as if embarrassed at having said too much. Nervously, he reached out the toe of his boot and crushed the fallen flower petal.

Dinah had trouble getting her breath. Her chest hurt. "How do I know this isn't a pack of lies?" she asked, her throat tight. "How do I know you aren't telling me this just because you don't like me?"

He put his hand in the breast pocket of his suit and drew out an envelope. "Because I got nothing to gain from it, ma'am," he said, meeting her eyes again. "This here's my resignation. Nashville can be a hard place. I'm used to playing rough. But I don't want to play as dirty as Mitch Carey, ma'am. So I'm givin' him what he wants. He's free of me, and it don't cost him a penny. But I wanted to apologize to you—and warn you. All he cares about is power. Well, he don't got it over me no more. Give him this for me, will you?"

He handed her the letter of resignation. She took it numbly. "And, ma'am," he said, "I ain't got no right to ask any favors of you. But I'd just as soon you didn't recount this conversation to him. He's a vengeful man. I want to work again. But not with him. I got a chance for a job in Los Angeles. I'd hate for him to ruin it. Would you mind not sayin' nothin'?''

Dinah looked first at the envelope in her hand, then at Lucky Bucky Williston, so huge yet seemingly so helpless. She didn't trust the man—but he had resigned. He had nothing to gain from lying. She made an instant decision, praying it was the right one.

"As far as I'm concerned, Mr. Williston," she said, "you gave me this letter and we said good-night. That's all."

He gave her a bow that would have been courtly had it not been so elephantine. "I thank you, ma'am," he said with dignity. "I hope you escape from this situation in better shape than I have."

He turned to leave. He had lumbered to the door when Dinah's voice stopped him. "Mr. Williston?"

He turned. His hat was on his head again, shading his little eyes. "Ma'am?"

"What about Roscoe? Is he . . . will he be . . . safe?"

Lucky Bucky's mouth took on an ugly ironic twist. "Mitch Carey don't aim to hurt the boy, miss. That boy is money in his pocket. He'll see that the kid has a right profitable career. Right profitable."

He turned again and waddled majestically from the sun room. But what about his life? Dinah wanted to cry after him. His career may be profitable, but will Mitch's schemes make him miserable?

But Lucky Bucky was gone. She looked at the envelope in her hand, not knowing what to do with it.

At last she decided to put the resignation letter in Mitch's study. She had never gone into the study before. She swung open the heavy door and went toward the oversize desk. She laid the envelope on the center of the blotter.

She couldn't help noticing a black-and-white photo in a heavy silver frame on the desk. The picture was of Vonda, and she looked ravishing, all thick, tumbling hair and dark doe eyes. In the corner, scribbled in a generous hand, was a note: "To Darling Mitch—My Gallant and My Cavalier—No One Could Do It Better. In Gratitude, Vonda."

The tightness in Dinah's throat threatened to choke her. She turned and fled from the room, running all the way up the curving stairs. She had to leave this place. But she couldn't abandon Roscoe. Not yet, with everything so uncertain and full of shadows.

SHE SLEPT POORLY and awoke just past dawn. Roscoe had a dental appointment at ten and an optometrist's appointment at two. She decided to let him sleep as late as possible. She sat alone on the patio, drinking tea she had made herself and nibbling a warmed-over muffin. It was so early that none of the servants were up. Even the birds still sounded sleepy.

She finished her tea and stared moodily at the bottom of the cup. She wished, helplessly, that one could truly read one's future in a teacup. Perhaps it was best she couldn't. Her future, unlike Roscoe's, looked none too bright.

She was startled from her reverie by the equivalent of a light but jolting electrical shock. A pair of warm lips grazed the back of her neck, lingered enticingly on her nape. A pair of strong hands closed around her upper arms. "Good morning," said Mitch's lazy, insinuating voice. "You didn't need to wait up for me."

She pulled in her chair and glared up at him. He stood behind her. He put his hands into his trouser pockets. He wore the same clothes he had on the night before. His black hair was tousled and a lock hung over one arched brow. He was unshaven. A slight smudge of lipstick was on his stubbled cheek, another on his unbuttoned collar. Dinah caught a whiff of whiskey mingled with expensive perfume. He must have been coming home from Vonda's bed, she thought bitterly.

"Stop kissing me on the neck," she ordered shortly and turned back to her muffin. It looked less appetizing than ever.

He smiled. He pulled out a chair and sat across from her. "I can't help myself. It's such a lovely neck. Well nigh irresistible. You should be glad I'm not a vampire."

"I'm not so sure you're not," she said, wondering why she could never breathe right when he was around.

"I couldn't be," he teased. "Look—here I sit in the light of the newly risen sun. No vampire could do that, could he?"

"I very much doubt you spent the night in a coffin with only some Transylvanian dust to keep you company, either," Dinah muttered, then bit her lip, wishing she had kept silent.

His smile only grew wider and more mocking. "You've got it backward. A vampire is supposed to spend his days, not his nights, in the coffin. Besides, what do you care how I spend my nights? Or where?"

"I don't in the least," she snapped. She gave him a covert glance. He looked as if he'd spent the night in total dissipation and had enjoyed it immensely. His green eyes were shadowed, but his grin was as irreverent and unsettling as ever.

"And did you have a nice well-bred chat on the phone with your fiancé? Was it exciting?"

She ignored his questions. She poured herself another cup of tea. "Lucky Bucky was here last night. He left a letter for you. It's in your study."

"Hmm," Mitch said, then yawned. He didn't seem in the least interested.

"He said it was important," she stated. She wished those long-lashed green eyes weren't trained on her with such indolent boldness.

"If I'm fortunate, he's resigning," he replied. He broke off a piece of her muffin and ate it. "I heard some poor fool in California might try to hire him. But I'm not sure I'm rid of him. He usually has one more trick up his sleeve."

Dinah looked at the handsome, unshaven face in frustration. Damn the man! Her news hadn't surprised him in the least. He always knew everything.

"Why are you up so early?" he asked, the grooves beside his mouth deepening. "It can't be that your conscience is bothering you. You're far too perfect for that. So it must be that rising at daybreak is the well-bred New England way of doing things right. Does your fiancé get up at crack of dawn, too? Does it keep him healthy, wealthy and wise? What does he do, anyway, besides let you run all over creation?"

"Dennis is in graduate school," she said stiffly. "When he gets out, he has family holdings to manage. But he'll also devote himself to music. In his spare time. As a professor."

She had thought, foolishly, that Mitch might be impressed. Instead he laughed aloud. "In his spare time? That's how your taste in men runs? To a professor whose real job is managing the family fortune? What a great, crashing bore. If only I'd known." He laughed again.

"Don't you have a civil bone in your body?" she asked in disgust.

"No," he replied with cynical cheer. "I don't. Do you have an uncivil one? What are your duties today, by the way? What genteel tortures do you have planned for Roscoe? Will I be able to have a moment or two of his time?"

She set down her teacup sharply, so it rang out when it made contact with the saucer. "Roscoe has appointments all day today," she said, tossing her golden bangs. "I have to see to his health, you know. You can talk to him this evening."

"Thank you very much," Mitch replied sarcastically. "You're too kind. You really are."

"I have to see to these things," Dinah countered in her own defense. "His eyes, especially, should have been taken care of long ago. I think he would have done much better in school if he'd had glasses. And you'll be keeping him busy all next week."

"Quite the concerned friend, aren't you?" Mitch gibed. "Or is it just your natural efficiency and no real affection at all?"

"Of course I have aff... affection for him," Dinah said, her small voice gruff.

"Good Lord," Mitch observed sourly, "you even have trouble saying the word *affection*. If it's hard for you to say, no wonder it's so difficult for you to feel. You really don't care what happens to this kid once your time with him is up, do you?"

"I certainly do!" she retorted. "I care a great deal."

There was a charged pause. They stared at each other across the table. Dinah realized she was breathing hard again and that her cheeks felt hot. Mitch's face was suddenly grim, his eyes hard above his shadowed jaw. It was as if some high-voltage cable ran sparking and humming dangerously between them.

She turned her face from his at last and looked off into the gardens. "You're going to keep him in Nashville, aren't you?" she said finally. "You'll offer him the contract, won't you? The demonstration tapes are only a formality, aren't they? He's going to be staying."

Another moment of magnetic force pulsed in the air. "Yes," Mitch replied at last. "He'll stay. What about you?"

Her eyes swung back to meet his. His gaze was not kind, tender or searching. It was stony. His face was rigid with lack of emotion. The outer corner of his left eye twitched slightly. That was all. Again she noticed the faint smear of lipstick on his cheek. His mouth was set in an unyielding line.

There he sat, disheveled and unshaven in the morning light, his hair falling into his eyes. His shirt was half-undone, showing the dark tangle of hair on his bronzed chest. He had been out all night, he had obviously been with Vonda Rainy and he not only looked unrepentant, he looked proud.

She should have hated him. But she wanted him so profoundly that she ached. She experienced emotions she was sure no MacNeil was ever intended to experience. MacNeils were taught to think rationally and to conform, not to feel such forbidden urges with such heart-shaking force.

"I can't stay here," she said woodenly. "I always told you that."

"You're really going back North," Mitch growled. "Back to him. The man who'll push the family stocks and bonds about? The money manager?"

She didn't answer directly. There had always been so much lying between them. She looked down at her ring and twisted it. "What's wrong with managing money?" she asked, hedging his question.

She felt his eyes raking over her. She heard his chair being pushed back, sensed him standing, staring down at her. "Nothing," he rasped. "I find it ironic. That's the kind of man you need to hold you in his arms. One content to handle a fortune somebody else made. Seems boring to me, but safe and sound to you, I suppose. What you want are things all wrapped up and neat. Settled from the beginning of time to its end.''

He strode away. She kept her eyes averted. She didn't even know what he'd meant. Nothing in her life was wrapped up and neat anymore. If he thought she didn't or couldn't feel, he was wrong. Completely wrong.

CHAPTER TEN

EVENTS BEGAN to crowd into one another at a pace that made Dinah light-headed. A thousand details and duties clamored for her attention.

Mitch was never far from her thoughts, though he was far away from her physically. He left Thursday night for business conferences in New York, and was gone the whole weekend. His absence haunted the house as formidably as his presence had.

He hadn't bothered to tell her where he was going or why. Mrs. Buttress, who came to the mansion to deliver some tapes, explained his disappearance matter-of-factly. He and Vonda Rainy had knotty negotiations to make with the company now holding her contract. They had flown, along with Vonda's agent and Mitch's lawyer, to the head office in Manhattan to wrangle with its executives.

Dinah was glad he was gone. The pain of knowing he was with Vonda was a clean, healthy kind of pain, she told herself. It taught her, with cutting finality, he was not the kind of man she could afford to love. He had already destroyed much of her orderly universe. If she let him, he would destroy it all, carelessly and with a smile.

She tried to lose herself in the minutiae of watching out for Roscoe. She took him to the dentist. She took him to the optometrist. She had him fitted for both regular glasses and contact lenses. She had his hair cut. She bought him more clothes. On Mrs. Buttress's orders, and with her assistance, she helped him buy a new guitar, charged to Mitch.

She listened to the tapes of studio recording artists that Mrs. Buttress had brought, and she helped Roscoe write down his opinions of them and their past performances. She triple-checked the reputations of everyone Mitch had recommended to work with Roscoe. She kept in touch with Vesta Hockenberry, assuring her that Roscoe was fine.

She set up a bank account and worked out a temporary budget for Roscoe and helped him send a check to Vesta, for he wanted to send home as much money as possible. In the meantime, she escorted him to every point of interest in Nashville, asking him all the time to teach her more about his music. They stayed up late, listening to records in the music room, studying them, analyzing them.

If Roscoe had worked this hard in school, Dinah thought sardonically, he would have already graduated from college as a prodigy. She lectured him gently, whenever she found an opening, on the importance of improving his education. He would only grin, showing her his improved smile, and tell her that he didn't need any more book-learnin'—he was doing what he liked best right now.

Mitch had not returned by Monday morning, when Dinah took Roscoe to the recording studio to begin rehearsing. Mrs. Buttress met them there and introduced them to the producer, Dick Winters, who, in turn, introduced them to a bewildering number of musicians, engineers, assistant engineers, mixers, editors and someone called a "project coordinator."

Roscoe peered nervously through his new contact lenses, shifted nervously on his new boots and smiled nervously with his new smile. He was ill at ease and frightened until the music actually began. Then he relaxed visibly, and Dinah relaxed, too. Mrs. Buttress kindly stayed by her to explain things.

"This is very unusual," Mrs. Buttress whispered in Dinah's ear, "taking this much trouble with a demonstration tape. I think Mr. Carey knows what he wants and that he plans to release these numbers as a test record. Roscoe does have the most extraordinary voice, you know."

Dinah nodded, smiling. She was just truly beginning to understand how special the boy's voice was.

"Mr. Carey looks on him as a diamond in the rough," confided Mrs. Buttress. "And that he is, in every sense. And Mr. Carey insists on nothing but the best for him. Of course, you mustn't let it go to the boy's head. I know you won't. You're far too sensible."

Dinah's smile faded. She no longer considered herself sensible in the least. And she knew somewhere, somehow, she had to find someone else to look out for Roscoe. But as she watched him singing so intently before his microphone, she felt a surge of pride swell over her heart like a great wave. He was doing so splendidly, she thought. He was blooming before her very eyes. And she had helped him—at least a little bit, hadn't she? She realized again how much she was going to miss him.

At five o'clock, the producer called it a day. Dinah breathed a sigh of relief. She and Mrs. Buttress left their little observation room to congratulate Roscoe. As Mrs. Buttress pumped his hand enthusiastically, Dinah affectionately held his thin arm, smiling up at him.

At that moment, Mitch Carey walked into the studio. Dinah's heart seemed to stop. She hadn't seen him for almost four days. His actual presence made her feel faint with happiness. Her mind jerked her emotions back sharply. She knew her face had gone pale, but she kept it blank.

He walked toward them casually. He wore black pants, a black linen shirt, and a subdued sport jacket of black-and-white glen plaid. He looked handsome, absolutely self-possessed, and slightly wicked. He nodded amiably at Mrs. Buttress, smiled at Roscoe, but ignored Dinah.

"Congratulations," he said to Roscoe, shaking his hand. "The producer said you made an amazing start."

Roscoe gulped, blushed and thanked him. He hid his embarrassment by putting his new guitar away with elaborate care.

"And how was your trip?" Mrs. Buttress questioned briskly. "Successful, I hope? You got Miss Rainy's contract difficulties cleared up?"

Mitch nodded. "She's mine now," he murmured nonchalantly. "All mine."

The cool satisfaction in his eyes made Dinah's heart feel withered.

"Splendid," replied Mrs. Buttress. "I'll have her new contract on your desk first thing tomorrow."

"No hurry." His green eyes flicked briefly to Dinah, then away in lack of interest. "She and her agent won't be back for another week or so. They've got some loose ends to tie up."

Mrs. Buttress clucked in sympathy. She waggled her graying head. "Well, I must say, we've all had quite a day. It was terribly exciting watching Roscoe. And nice to get out of the office. It can feel a little confining, especially with the construction."

"And how is the construction going?" Mitch asked her, arching a dark brow in concern. "No more mice, I hope."

Dinah felt her cheeks darkening at his words. He didn't seem to notice.

"Indeed not!" returned Mrs. Buttress with some spirit. "You told me to take care of the mouse problem. You may therefore consider the mouse problem taken care of. Or my name is not Adelle Cappington Buttress.''

He smiled, an easy white smile that made Dinah's heart race treacherously. ''Thoughtless of me, Mrs. Buttress. Pretend I never asked.''

''Done,'' she replied crisply. ''Now I'm off to get a bite to eat. Unless you need me for something else.''

''Actually, I'd like you to take Roscoe out for supper,'' he told her. He opened his wallet and handed her several bills. ''Someplace nice. To reward you both.''

Mrs. Buttress handed him back some of the bills. ''It doesn't do to spoil either of us,'' she admonished him. ''Also, throwing money about sets a poor example for the young man. We'll dine well, but modestly, thank you. And I'll bring you the change. Come, Roscoe.''

The older woman bustled Roscoe out of the studio, shooing him like a gangling chick before her.

''Hmm,'' Mitch mused, looking after them. ''She's exhibiting even more military discipline than usual. It must be your influence.''

He turned, letting his eyes rest on Dinah for the first time. Looking up into that mysteriously green stare, she no longer felt in complete control of herself.

''I have no influence.'' She kept her voice even and without emotion.

''But you have,'' he contradicted, smiling the slightest bit. ''It's certainly showing on Roscoe. He looks sensational. What have you done?''

''Nothing, really,'' she answered. ''Just the things that needed to be done.'' She started toward the door.

''Wait,'' he said. He made no move to stop her, but his voice was as effective as a physical barrier. ''I'll take you to dinner.''

She refused to turn to face him. "No, thank you. I don't care to."

"Dinah." His tone was sharp with warning. "I want to talk to you. About Roscoe, of course."

"You'll have to make an appointment," she answered curtly. "I've already put in a full day."

"Dammit!" He stepped in front of her. He put his lean, tanned hands on her upper arms. He made a movement almost as if he would shake her, but squared his shoulders instead. The vein in his temple danced dangerously. "I said that I want to talk to you. Now will you behave yourself and come with me?"

She looked up into his implacable face. "I said I didn't want to. I—I need some time to myself."

"You've had nearly four days to yourself," he said between his teeth. "You never even said hello." His mouth crooked slightly, relieving the intensity of his expression. "What's the matter? Aren't you glad to see me?"

She looked around the studio helplessly. Everyone else had disappeared. She hated what the touch of his hands on her arms was doing to her. "Why should I be glad to see you? Why, for that matter, should either of us be glad to see the other?"

The mocking smile seemed to freeze on his lips. His touch suddenly felt charged with tension. "Why? You're right. No reason at all. We seem to have an almost supernatural talent for getting under each other's skin. But I have some questions. And you have answers. So you might as well bear with me."

"What questions?" She lifted her chin higher. "Ask them here."

He studied her for a long moment, then let his hands fall away, turning from her brusquely. He ran a hand through his black hair. "First," he muttered, "about Roscoe. The dentist, the eye doctor, all this stuff. He looks great. But who's paying for it?"

"I am," she answered. "But I told him you are. That it's in his contract. All right, it's a lie, but he needs all these things done and he can't afford it. Not yet, anyway. It's something I can do for him. And he wouldn't take an outright present."

He wheeled to face her. His mouth was taut with irony. "You lied to him. I can't believe it. You actually did something immoral, Dinah. For a good cause, of course. Good Lord, is that all you think you can do for the boy—give him a little health care and a haircut? Can't you see you represent something more important to him? I'll pay you back for everything. I insist."

"I won't accept. I did it on my own. It's my responsibility."

"You're impossible," he said in disgust. "Are you even listening to what I'm saying?"

She crossed her arms protectively and looked at him in wary defiance. "You're paying for the guitar, of course. I'm sorry Roscoe didn't thank you properly for it, but he will tomorrow. He was exhausted, and you took him by surprise."

"I'm not interested in thank-yous," he began. He stalked to the back of the studio and stood by the drum set, looking at it as if he were deciding whether to kick it.

"I am," she asserted. "I don't want him neglecting common courtesy, for heaven's sake."

He glowered at the drums and heaved an exasperated sigh. He moved away from them, as if they offered too much temptation to vent his emotions. "Who's going to keep track of his thank-yous when you're gone?" he asked, standing before her again. "You're still going, I suppose."

An invisible line seemed to divide the two of them. To cross it, she realized, would be perilous. "Of course, I'm going. As soon as possible."

"And who'll look out for him then?" he challenged, his eyes smoldering.

"I don't know yet," she bit out. "I'll find someone."

"I can't do it, you know," he stated. "It's a full-time job. I've got a record company to run. I can't spend all my time chaperoning some teenager."

"I don't expect you to. Nor do I expect you to go on being his host. I'm sure it puts a crimp in your life-style, and as Mrs. Buttress pointed out, he could have a better example than you."

He tossed an angry glance around the room, as if once again he was looking for something to break. "Naturally he can't stay indefinitely. But as long as you're there with him it's not a problem," he said.

"I'm looking for another place," she told him. She took a deep breath. "As soon as he's signed that contract and has his own money, I'll see that he's put up somewhere that's more appropriate."

"Dammit, Dinah!"

"Among other things, he has to learn to pay his own way, doesn't he?" she asked, staring up at his angry face. "The same as all of us."

"Dammit!" he swore again. "You're going to stand there and talk about money? The two of you don't have to leave. There's a lot more at stake here than money. Will you get that through your head?"

"Don't swear," she ordered, which made him swear again. "I know what's involved," she insisted. "Responsibility, for one thing. He has to take some eventually. All I wish is that I could get him to go back and finish his schooling."

"He's going to be rich," Mitch said almost savagely. "He's going to be famous. What does he need to go back to school for?"

"For his own good," Dinah shot back. "And don't tell me you don't understand. Or would you prefer to keep him uneducated so you can manipulate him more neatly?"

"I've never manipulated him," Mitch growled. "Never. And you know what else? I've never met a woman who can make me as mad as you do. What is it? A gift you've got, or what?"

"You don't make me any happier than I make you," she responded. "There must be a moral here somewhere—and I imagine that it's that we stay as far from each other as possible."

"That's fine. That's fine," he said with a sort of grim satisfaction. "You stay out of my way and I'll stay out of yours."

"Fine," she echoed. "Just fine." Her breath was ragged. She held herself as tall as possible and started toward the door once more. Her knees felt numb and weak, but she managed to walk as proudly as a princess.

"Hey!" he said sharply. She turned. He reached into his breast pocket and drew out a small package. "I brought you something from New York. You might as well have it. I've got no need for it."

"I don't—" she began, but he cut her off.

"I said take it," he grated. He tossed the little box to her unceremoniously, and gave her a contemptuous look.

She could bear to argue with him no further. She thrust the package into her purse and didn't bother him with the insincerity of a thank-you. She swept out of the studio.

It wasn't until that night that she dared to open the box. Mitch, in spite of his long trip, had never come back to the mansion. Dinah had spent the evening with Roscoe, who was practicing for his next session.

When she finally retired she sat staring moodily at the box in its white wrapping. At last she steeled herself to strip away the delicate paper.

She drew her breath in sharply. The box was from Tiffany's. Within was a pin of gold, diamonds and sapphires—a perfect, tiny jeweled mousetrap.

With tears in her eyes she rewrapped it as best she could. She took paper and pen and wrote a note in as steady a hand as she was able. "Mr. Carey," she wrote, "it would be totally inappropriate for me to accept such an expensive gift. Please do not let us speak any more about this matter. Dinah MacNeil." She folded the note and thrust it into an envelope.

She went downstairs and gave the little box and the envelope to one of the maids and asked that it be put on Mitch's desk.

She went back to her room. She spent a long time staring out the window at the garden awash with silver moonlight. She supposed the note sounded foolish, terse and old-fashioned, but she knew she had no other choice. She couldn't keep the pin. It would make her think of him. And she had to learn to stop doing that. She needed to forget his laughing cynicism, his strong arms, the mastery of his kisses. She hoped he would never bring up the diamond mousetrap again.

She needn't have worried. He didn't speak of it. After that, he hardly spoke to her at all.

THE TAPING SESSIONS went on for another three days. Mitch appeared frequently at the studio. He encouraged Roscoe, the producer, the engineers. He ignored Dinah. When she had a question for him, he looked right through her and muttered, "Ask Mrs. Buttress. She's the most efficient woman in Nashville. She knows as much about it as I do." Then he would walk away.

Where he was spending his nights, Dinah didn't know, but he was seldom home before four in the morning. Dinah had started spending her lunch hours with Mrs. Buttress, who ate in her office. Roscoe and the musicians usually had food sent in. Dinah, locked out of their growing camaraderie, picked up a sandwich and coffee and went to join Mrs. Buttress.

"Roscoe's going to be given the contract tomorrow," Mrs. Buttress said, wiping sawdust off a chair so Dinah could sit. "It's still exactly the same as the copy you were shown. I don't know why Mr. Carey couldn't tell you that. I don't know what's wrong with that man at all, in fact. He's as touchy as a bear with a sore paw these days."

Dinah sat down gingerly and took the lid off her coffee. "He...he's been staying out very late," she said.

Mrs. Buttress looked at her intently. "Oh, he has, has he?" she asked suspiciously. "With whom could he be? He's made a point of being seen with Miss Rainy, but she's in New York.... Well, he must have found someone else. I never did believe the stories about him and Miss Rainy—although stranger things have happened in this town, I'll warrant."

Dinah's emotions sank. Was Mitch so hot-blooded that he couldn't even wait for Vonda to get back from New York? He had to find someone else to spend his nights with?

"Not that I'd blame Miss Rainy for wanting him," Mrs. Buttress intoned, unwrapping her own sandwich. "The woman could use some stability in her life. Her previous taste in men has been quite atrocious. Leeches and weaklings. Mr. Carey would be a welcome change."

"They make a handsome couple," Dinah said tonelessly, trying to hide her sadness. "But he shouldn't be running around behind her back."

"Well," Mrs. Buttress said philosophically. "He won't be running about next week. Next week he has to see to that young woman from Canada. She's playing hard to get, and she'll take all his energy. She'll be staying at the mansion. I'm sure he told you."

"No," Dinah replied, her spirits sinking still lower. Another woman still? That sounded excessive even for Mitch Carey. But she had been warned. Then, before she lost her nerve she said, "I need to find Roscoe a place of his own. He can't go on staying with Mr. Carey forever."

"Certainly not," agreed Mrs. Buttress. "It would imply favoritism on Mr. Carey's part."

"I need to find him an apartment as soon as he signs that contract," Dinah continued. "And I haven't had time to do anything—and it's so hard."

"Your needs are certainly difficult," Mrs. Buttress observed with scientific interest. "You need a place to accommodate both the boy and yourself."

"But I won't be staying forever," Dinah hastened to add.

"So Mr. Carey keeps saying," said the older woman. "He tells me every day with the most annoying regularity. Though who you'll get to take your place I don't know."

"I don't, either," Dinah murmured unhappily. "But first, I have to find him—us—a place, and I just don't—"

Mrs. Buttress neatly wiped her lips clean of the last vestiges of her sandwich. "I'm surprised," she muttered thoughtfully, "that Mr. Carey never mentioned I have rooms to rent."

"You?" Dinah asked.

"Ever since my youngest son left home," Mrs. Buttress answered. Sadness tinged her brisk voice. "The house is so big. It seems empty. That's why I went back to work full-time. I miss the boys. Roscoe reminds me of my middle boy, Darrell. Such a sweet nature. But one had to look out for him all the time—so easily taken advantage of. He's an intern now. In Walla Walla.''

Dinah's sandwich froze midair, halfway to her mouth. Small bells began to flash in her head. Sirens went off. Lights began to flash.

She set down the sandwich. She looked Mrs. Buttress in the eye. "Mrs. Buttress," she said, with all the canniness of a true MacNeil, "I have a business proposition for you."

At that moment she knew she was finally going to escape Nashville. Escaping her hopeless love for Mitch Carey was another and more difficult problem. But she was taking the first step. And as a sage had said, that is how the longest and most arduous journey must begin—with a first step.

CHAPTER ELEVEN

EIGHT DAYS LATER Dinah could see the gray Atlantic spread out beneath her as her plane descended toward Boston's Logan International Airport. In the past, she had always felt as if she was coming home when she saw that foaming coast. Now all she felt was emptiness.

She looked at the strange object in her hands. The stewardesses and other passengers had bestowed furtive glances on her for carrying it. It was Roscoe's old oversize white hat, his lucky hat. At the Nashville airport, he had insisted she take it. Hugging him goodbye, she had nearly wept.

"If you'd stay," Roscoe had muttered in a choked voice, holding her awkwardly, "I'd go back to school. I swear it."

She pulled away, smiling mistily at him. "That's blackmail, Roscoe. You should go back no matter what. Shouldn't he, Mrs. Buttress?"

"Yes, he should, and I'll do my best to see he does," Mrs. Buttress said. She gave Dinah a surprisingly warm embrace. "I'll watch out for him. And I'll call his mother twice a week, and get him home for all the holidays."

"I know you will." Dinah nodded solemnly, staring at the big hat in her hands. She had swallowed hard. Then the second announcement came for the boarding of her plane and she turned abruptly from the two of them. She could not bear to stretch the goodbye out any longer.

"So long," she said, her voice shaky. She picked up her travel bag and walked away, vowing not to look back.

"Thank you!" shouted Roscoe's voice from behind her. "Miss MacNeil—thank you!"

"No," she called, without turning. She kept walking swiftly. "Thank you, Roscoe. Thanks for everything." Her voice had broken.

Now she stared moodily out the window as the plane sailed closer to its appointed runway. Her heart already ached with longing for the flash and excitement of Nashville, for Roscoe and Mrs. Buttress, and most of all for Mitch.

But it was over now. She had done her duty. Roscoe's contract was signed. He was, according to all opinions, on his way to being a star. And he was taken care of.

He had moved in a few days before with Mrs. Buttress. He had his own room, but Mrs. Buttress treated him like one of her own sorely missed sons and gave him the run of the house. Dinah had stayed with them until she left for Boston. She knew that at last Roscoe was in good, honest and totally capable hands.

The only shadow on the picture was Mitch. He had accosted her in the sun room the night before she and Roscoe were to move to Mrs. Buttress's.

"This is a new low," he said between his teeth. His hand on her arm was almost painful. "Not only are you walking out on the kid, you're stealing my secretary. You're the same pirate they say you're great-grandfather was."

Dinah drew away, careful not to show him how profoundly his touch shook her. "You can always find another secretary," she retorted. "Where else can I find someone to look after Roscoe? Somebody who knows this business—and you and all your tricks?"

"My tricks?" he snarled. "What about your tricks? How much did you offer her, anyway, to steal her away?"

Dinah raised her chin in challenge. "Fifty dollars a week raise. Plus a percentage of Roscoe's earnings. One half percent of what he clears. And it's a bargain, believe me. His mother and Willard and the lawyers agree."

His jaw clenched in anger. "A percentage! Good Lord, where'd you come up with that idea, you lacy little buccaneer?"

"From being in Nashville. And around this business," Dinah retorted. "And don't you dare take this out on Mrs. Buttress. It's a marvelous opportunity for her. You worked the woman unmercifully."

"I don't hold it against Mrs. Buttress," he muttered harshly. "I hold it against you. Does your fiancé know what a hardheaded little businesswoman he's getting? Or is that what makes your blood so blue? Your absolute ruthlessness?"

She could say nothing. He walked away. He had business with the woman from Canada. She had just arrived and was dark haired, dimpled, beautiful and eager to please.

THE PLANE'S WHEELS thumped against the runway. Dinah shook her head to clear it. Dennis would be meeting her. They had continued their regularly scheduled telephone calls, but each conversation was emptier than the last. He had offered to be there when her plane arrived. But the decision to part had been made.

The airport had never looked so impersonal. With her carry-on case in one hand and Roscoe's battered hat in the other, she began the long hike toward the waiting area.

When she saw Dennis's round face with its pale mustache, she tried to smile but couldn't. Normally cheerful to a fault, he didn't seem able to smile, either. "Welcome back, Di-Di," he said, pecking her mechanically on the cheek. He cast a suspicious look at the Stetson in her hand. "What's that thing?"

"A hat," she said sharply, because tears were choking her throat. "And Dennis, I don't think I'm Di-Di anymore. That's a little girl's name."

He looked at her apprehensively. "You've changed," he accused. He looked unnaturally solemn, as if for the first time in his life he was taking something seriously.

"You've changed, too," she said softly.

"Yes. Well." Dennis took her bag. He seemed ill at ease. "Let's get a drink. I need one."

They settled into one of the many cocktail lounges that Logan housed. They looked at each other. There seemed to be nothing to say. Dinah shrugged unhappily. She took off her ring. She handed it to Dennis, who accepted it without protest. "I'm sorry," she murmured.

Dennis put the ring neatly into a box and put the box into his pocket. He took a large sip of his martini. "Don't be sorry," he told her and glanced nervously about the lounge. He bent closer to her conspiratorially. "It's for the best. We were never suited to be man and wife. I realized that long ago, Dinah. I thought we could get along, somehow. It would have made other people happy, but not us. It would have been a disaster."

Dinah relaxed slightly against the leather banquette. "I'm glad you understand—" she began.

He cut her off. "Dinah, I got married."

"What?" She sat upright, her eyes widening with horror and disbelief.

His round face was crimson. "I got married. Her name is Bella. She's a show girl." He forced himself to meet Dinah's disbelieving eyes. "I've been seeing girls like that for years. I couldn't let Mother know. It's why I was hardly ever home at nights. I thought I could keep it up after we were married and you wouldn't know or be hurt. I mean, lots of men do it, and you just never seemed very interested in me that way. Physically, I mean.''

"Married?" Dinah gasped. "You got married?"

"Shh!" Dennis warned, leaning closer and putting his finger to his mustache. "I thought you'd probably be getting married yourself—to that person in Nashville. I didn't want it to look like I...well...wasn't man enough for you. I know it seems like foolish pride to you, Dinah, but I'd rather be thought a cad than a fool. I've faced my lusty appetites at last. Mother's just going to have to accept that it's girls like Bella who attract me. I haven't told Mother yet. I want you to come with me and tell her you don't really mind and you know it's for the best. Will you?"

"Dennis," Dinah uttered in shock. "Help you tell your mother? After you made me promise to keep wearing your ring? And not to tell anyone I wanted to break the engagement? After having me live a lie?"

Dennis turned redder. He took another long pull from his martini. "It was just a little lie, Dinah. For just a little while. I needed time to think. And when you see Bella, you'll know I've made the right decision. What a woman, Dinah! She's six feet tall! Long legged, and she looks wonderful in black net stockings and spike heels. And in leather she's simply smashing."

"Dennis, you're unbelievable," she said, staring at him. "If I weren't a reasonable person—"

"You don't know how hard it's been," he practically wailed in his own defence. "How I hated playing that blasted harp to please Mother. But it did give me an excuse to spend time the way I wanted—with great tall leggy girls like Bella. You and I never found each other physically attractive, Dinah. For years you were just this tiny thing with a bad cold. Frankly, I didn't think you could feel physically attracted to any man. But now we've both found someone else. So you can tell Mother that—"

Dinah rose and snatched up Roscoe's hat. "Tell your mother by yourself, Dennis," she interrupted. "Be a man about it for once in your life. And don't bother to drive me home. I'll rent a car."

"Dinah!" Dennis pleaded. "Don't be childish. What difference does it make if you wore the ring a few weeks longer? It kept our parents happy and it gave me time to think. It's not as if it really meant anything. You don't really love me, so it's nothing to get emotional about."

"Don't stop me from being emotional, Dennis," she admonished hotly. She seized her purse and case. "I'm just learning to be emotional. It's taken a long time, but I think I'm getting the hang of it."

She turned on her heel and left. She clenched her jaw to keep from crying, but tears blurred her vision as she strode through the concourse. She'd never understood Dennis in the least. He had been unfaithful all along, would have married her and kept on being unfaithful, without a qualm. She'd been a perfect fool. How Mitch would laugh if he knew. Mitch, she though with anguish. Mitch. She could see him smiling now.

SOMEHOW DINAH'S MOTHER believed Dennis's marriage to Bella was Dinah's fault. "If only you hadn't gone to Nashville," her mother mourned. "It changed you. Dennis said it had. No wonder he ran off and did this."

Dinah refused to discuss Dennis or Nashville. She didn't mention Mitch Carey. Instead she told her family she neither wanted to go to Yale nor work in the steel museum. She would find another teaching job; it was the only career that interested her. The atmosphere of the house was icy.

"All you do is mope and listen to that dreadful country music," her mother fumed. "Did you have an affair in Nashville? Dennis claims you did. Something's certainly changed you. Is that it?"

"No," Dinah answered, turning away. "I didn't have an affair." *But I wish I had,* she thought bitterly.

At last her mother and Dennis's mother decided to console themselves by going on a shopping trip to New York. Her father went to New Hampshire with two other judges to angle for salmon and argue law around the campfire.

Dinah drifted aimlessly around the house, with only the servants for company. She listened incessantly to the country-western station in Boston, as if it could transport her back to Nashville. She thought of Roscoe and Mrs. Buttress and the horrible mansion and the beautiful villa. Mostly she thought about Mitch. Images of him played through her mind all day and half the night. She wondered which of the women he had held last in his arms. Vonda? The beautiful brunette from Canada? The mysterious woman with whom he'd spent so many nights when Vonda was gone?

One cool sunny morning a letter from Roscoe arrived. Delighted, she took it into the formal garden, unfolding it with hands that trembled, wondering if he had written anything about Mitch.

"Dear Miss MacNeil," the letter began in Roscoe's laborious handwriting.

We are fine. We went home to see my ma and sisters. They are fine. Mr. Carey is fine. Nashville is fine. My album is done. Everybody says it is fine. Vonda Rainy got married. She is fine. Please come see us. I miss you. I hope you are fine.

Yours truly,

Your Very Good Friend Forever,
Roscoe Ralph Hockenberry, Jr.

P.S. I can read better with these glasses. I read a book
about Hank Williams. It was fine. I miss you. I hope
you are fine.

Dinah sat up with a jolt when she read that Vonda Rainy
was married. To whom? Surely not to Mitch, or Roscoe
would have said, wouldn't he? She reread the letter three
times. How like Roscoe, she thought in frustration, to be
able to communicate anything in a song but nothing in a
letter. Mitch was "fine." What did that mean?

She was startled when the cook, Svetla, appeared just
behind her chair.

"Excuse it, please," said Svetla, her brow furrowed. "But
a man wants to see you. I don't know who. But I think he is
a workman, a repairman, something like that."

Hastily Dinah folded the letter and thrust it into her skirt
pocket. "What does he want?" she asked distractedly. She
didn't really care. She wanted to read the letter again, looking between the lines for any information about Mitch.

"I don't know what he wants," Svetla said, shaking her
head. "He looks like a gentleman, but his business sounds
most strange."

"Why?" Dinah asked.

Svetla gave an elaborate shrug. "He said he come about
the mousetrap. I should let him to see you? Yes? No?"

Dinah's heart took flight and winged away from her so
swiftly that she was breathless. "Yes," she said. "Please."

Svetla padded off.

It can't be, Dinah thought dazedly. But it was. In a moment Mitch stood at the garden's edge, the French doors of
the dining room behind him.

He wore a white suit with a white shirt unbuttoned at the collar. His hair was blacker than she remembered, his skin more bronzed. But his eyes were still the same hypnotic and electric green that haunted her dreams.

She stood. Unthinkingly she put her hand to her breast so that it rested on the tiny ruffles of her sleeveless blouse.

Neither of them said hello. They simply looked at each other. He took two steps toward her, then stopped. He raised his chin slightly as he appraised her. His head cocked. One dark brow quirked higher than normal. His usual taunting mouth was a grim line. She felt the pounding of her pulse.

At last he smiled. It was a sardonic smile, as maddening as she remembered. "Well," he said in his lazy voice. "So you didn't marry him. I just heard. It takes a while for the Connecticut social notes to get to Tennessee."

"Yes," Dinah said, looking away. "He married someone else."

"I always said he was a fool," he scoffed.

"It's all right. He and I were never right for each other."

There was a beat of silence. "Too bad you didn't know that in Nashville."

She met his eyes again with her dark blue ones. "I did know." Somehow she kept the quaver out of her voice.

"Oh," he replied casually. "You just weren't interested in the local talent, eh?"

"What?" she asked. The familiar trembling she'd felt so often in his presence overtook her again.

"The local talent. Me," he said evenly, his smile suddenly seeming forced. "You weren't interested in me. Can't say that I blame you. It was too sudden. And I came on too strong, expecting you'd feel the same. I guess I was used to taking what I wanted and offering no explanation. Sorry."

"There's nothing to be sorry about," she said in confusion. "Won't you sit down? Do you want a drink? How's Roscoe? I just got a letter from him. He says he read a book. I couldn't be more thrilled. Except, of course, if he'd go back to school. Maybe he will. He said Vonda Rainy got married. But he didn't say to whom. Was it you?"

He didn't sit. He simply stood, his stare riveted on her. "Vonda and I? You're chattering, Dinah," he admonished. "Don't be ridiculous. Just give me an answer. How about it?"

She stared at him in confusion. "How about what?"

He stepped closer to her. He put his hands on her upper arms. "About us? Now that the ring is finally off your finger?"

She turned her face but was powerless to move away. "I only wore the ring as a courtesy," she said, then bit her lip. "I—I knew long ago something was wrong between Dennis and me. I'd promised him I'd wait until I was home to break it off. So we could talk."

"That's not what I asked you."

He took her chin between his thumb and forefinger and turned her face back to his. "I asked you about us. The two of us."

"I wasn't aware there was a two of us," she said shakily. "I thought there were three or four or five of us. That you had more than your share of women."

His smile was gone. "There was nobody but you from the moment I saw you. I wanted only you, Dinah. I wasn't prepared for it to happen, but it did, and I wanted you more than I wanted anything in my life. I still do, and I always will. That's why I came."

She stared up at him helplessly. Tears welled in her eyes. "But I heard so many things," she protested. "About you and Vonda—"

His hands tightened on her arms, drawing her closer to him. The warmth of his fingers seemed like fire on her bare flesh. "Vonda and I are business. We're friends, too. She cried on my shoulder after her last nervous collapse, and before this marriage. I held her hand and that was it."

"Collapse?" she asked, bewildered. "And marriages? I never heard any of that. I heard she was going to marry you."

His gaze dwelt on her trembling lips. "It takes a while to know the real secrets in a town," he said. "And people like Vonda know how to keep rumors quiet as long as possible. One way is to let other rumors circulate. I helped her through one collapse. That's when she stayed with me. Stories about us started, but they helped her hide her engagement. She asked me if I minded if her name was linked with mine—it helped her keep her real life private. I hadn't met you then. I agreed to be a sort of cavalier for her, a decoy. Once I'd given my promise to her, I couldn't break it. And you gave the impression that you didn't care, even though I thought it was obvious that it was you I loved."

Dinah looked at him questioningly.

He gave a short, humorless laugh. "Good grief," he muttered. "How could I love her? She's too flamboyant, too excitable, too unstable. You couldn't really think—"

"But I thought you were seeing someone else, too," Dinah objected, much as she wanted to believe he spoke the truth. "You were out almost every night when Vonda was gone."

"Oh," he mumbled. "That." For the first time since she had known him he showed signs of embarrassment. "I was trying to forget you. It didn't work. I thought you really were going to come back here and marry that idiot. I ended up every night at the new mansion. I'd play gin rummy with Troutman, talk about how unreasonable women were and drink too much. Do you realize that never in my life have I drunk too much? Until I thought I couldn't have you. That's how crazy I was, wanting you.''

"But all the rumors..." Dinah said uncertainly. "And then you had the Canadian girl come stay with you..."

Although she was afraid to trust him, she found she was resting one hand on his chest and that her finger was tracing the top of his shirt pocket. She had to touch him; she could not help herself.

"Don't tell me you were actually jealous, Dinah," he said, smiling. "It would mean that there might be hope for me," he said, nuzzling her golden hair. "If you got to know the Canadian lady, you'd hear all about the musician in Toronto that she loves. As for the rumors—I told you. They were only rumors. Vonda needed privacy and time to heal. We set up a smoke screen, that's all. She got married secretly in New York. To a very sensible man. I think she's going to be happy at last."

His voice became husky as his lips moved against her ear. "Dinah, nobody mattered but you. Can't you feel it? I would have told you in Nashville, only I was too proud, too angry at the thought you loved someone else. If I couldn't have you, at least I could have my pride. But pride's a terrible bedfellow—cold as death. And you're as warm in my arms as life itself. Come back to Nashville with me."

She pulled back slightly, though she wanted to melt into him, to stop fighting and simply to become one with him. He began to slowly lower his mouth to hers. She gave a little gasp of pleasure, but she managed to say, "But Lucky Bucky said—"

"What?" he asked in disbelief. "What's he got to do with this? He was one of Bobby's legacies. An unfortunate one."

"He said you and Vonda—" The light in his eyes made her incapable of finishing the sentence. "He said you'd set Roscoe against her and all of us against one another."

"Lucky Bucky is a vengeful fool," he muttered. "If he told you anything, it was to make trouble. He's a vain and petty man who's famous for getting even. If he couldn't sue me, he'd get at me however he could. He must have sensed how I felt about you. He's got a certain animal cunning in him, and a malicious streak a mile wide. He'd want to ruin any sort of relationship between us—business or personal."

"You mean he simply lied?" Dinah asked in horror. "For the sheer pleasure of it?"

"Creating trouble is second nature to an egoist like Bucky," Mitch almost growled. "I'd gotten rid of him and you'd made a fool of him. I imagine he couldn't rest if he thought he hadn't revenged himself somehow. But I don't want to talk about him. Kiss me, Dinah. Or the wanting to will kill me."

She yielded to the seduction in his voice and eyes. His lips bore down on hers again in a dizzying combination of tenderness and relentless demand. His tongue tasted like warm, magical wine against her own. His hands moved to her back, pulling her to him more intimately. The hardness of his chest pressed against the yearning tips of her breasts.

"I love you, Dinah," he breathed. "I love your strength and your beauty and your delicacy and your integrity. I hope you can learn to love me back. Even if I don't deserve it."

Her arms circled his neck, and her lips wanted the bruising pleasure of his again. "I don't have to learn to love you," she whispered achingly. "I knew how to do it from the first. Without even knowing who or what you were. Is that insane?"

He sombered, gathered his self-control. "When you know all about me you may not want me. I know your family won't approve. There's much I haven't told you. It may affect how you feel. We come from very different backgrounds, Dinah. Your family's been distinguished for generations. Mine's still struggling to produce a good streak of plain old respectability."

"I don't think respectability has anything to do with how I feel," Dinah said happily, laying her cheek against his throat. She could feel his vibrant strength.

He ran his hand through the gold silk of her hair. "Bobby was always the one the past haunted. I thought I was immune—until I met you," he said in a low voice. He drew back slightly and put his hand beneath her chin, turning her face up to him. His expression was sober, almost severe. "Nobody in Nashville knows much about Bobby and me. You'll see why. It's complicated, and it's not pleasant. Tell me, did you ever hear of a record company called Gemstone?"

Dinah looked up into his serious emerald gaze. She shook her head. "Gemstone Records? No. I don't think so."

A grim smile crooked one corner of his mouth. "My father started it. Forty years ago. And he destroyed it—twenty years ago. A payola scandal—payoffs and bribery. It was one of the biggest scandals in the music industry. He ruined not only himself but a couple of hundred other people. He went to prison. He died there. His name was Johnny Dark. Needless to say, it's not a name that inspires confidence within the industry."

"I—I'm sorry," Dinah whispered, studying the stern lines bracketing his mouth.

"Dinah," he murmured harshly, drawing her closer. "My father was a very rich man. He was much older than my mother. She was an aspiring singer. She'd grown up poor.

She was never happy with my father, but she thought he could give her security. She was wrong."

A line etched itself between his brows, and his jawline was rigid. Dinah shyly put her hand to his tensed cheek muscles. "My father came up the hard way, Dinah. He went to California from Tennessee, in fact—Knoxville. He built an empire and then he lost it. I was eleven. Bobby was nine. My mother was humiliated. She divorced him while he was in prison and married another man, almost as rich as my father had been. Alvin Carey. He adopted Bobby and me. And he never let us forget for a minute what a favor he'd done us and what a loser he thought our father was. And of course Mother, burnt by the music business once, didn't want Bobby or me to have anything to do with it."

His hand covered hers, pressing it more tightly against his face. He shook his ruefully. "But something odd happened. My father had invested in a small little-known record company in my mother's name. My mother wanted to sell it, but my stepfather, who was nobody's fool, wouldn't let her. He was right. The company turned out to be magic—it eventually became Mecca Records. And it made more money than my mother had ever thought possible. When my stepfather had a stroke, she needed me to see to the family business interests. I'd been teaching economics at Berkeley."

He laughed harshly. "I mocked your fiancé for managing the family wealth and being a professor on the side." He paused and kissed the palm of her hand. "But that's exactly what I'd done. The irony that you were going to marry a man just like I used to be was a little too much. But watching Mecca's workings from a distance left me hungry, somehow. It didn't seem like enough. It made me realize I wanted to build something on my own. Then Bobby died—and there was Diamond Horseshoe, waiting."

He kissed her wrist lightly. "For years, I played the dutiful son. But Bobby was rebellious from the start. He and my stepfather hated each other. Bob was ashamed of our real father and defiant about him at the same time. And of course, he wanted to make it in music on his own, one way or another. Mother did everything in her power to discourage him, including threatening to disown him. He was determined to make a go of it—without owing one blasted thing to the family or cashing in on his connection to Mecca. That's when he made a bid for Diamond Horseshoe."

"And that's why nobody in Nashville knew much about him?" Dinah asked.

He sighed roughly. He laid her cheek against his chest again. "He refused to mention the family's share of Mecca. He didn't dare say anything about our real father—the name is still poison in this business. Bobby seemed doomed to make a disaster of everything he touched—until Diamond Horseshoe. I'd studied the business. And I had instincts. I sensed Bobby'd finally found his great opportunity—if he could settle down. But he died. He was always troubled. Always. And he was drunk the night he took off in that light plane. My mother still can't talk about it. And won't."

He hugged her so tightly that her ribs hurt. She could sense the conflicts within him. "I'd wanted him to make it, Dinah. I loved him, but I was angry with him for always rebelling—even against me—and for dying. It was such a stupid thing for him to do—to die. It didn't have to happen. Maybe I'm just starting to forgive him now. It's strange, but I really was angry. That he let himself die."

He was silent a moment. His jaw rested against the silky sweep of her hair. "I came to Nashville and discovered what a mess he'd made—hiring Lucky Bucky, for one thing. And I was hooked by the end of the first day. I saw Bobby might be dead, but his dream could live. So I took over the company. To make it a success for him—and for myself. And to admit that for good or bad, music was in my blood. To show the world that a son of Johnny Dark could make it in this business without any favors from Mecca Records—or anybody else. Mother had to hire someone to look after the family assets.''

"You're estranged from your family, then?'' she asked, tracing the determined line beside his mouth.

"No, love. Not estranged. They're waiting for me to fail, as my father did and as Bobby did. They're beginning to realize I won't. They'll have to swallow some pride, that's all. But, as you can see, love hasn't done well in my family. That's why I avoided it until now. Until you. You'll have to know, my blood isn't blue, and my past isn't spotless, Dinah. My family history leaves much to be desired. But I'm Johnny Dark's son—no more, no less.''

She understood now. He had gone to Nashville to show the world that Bobby Carey could have been a success. And he had gone to meet his destiny, come to terms with his past, without favors from anyone.

"Johnny Dark fathered a very wonderful son,'' she said, her voice quavering. She looked up at him and tightened her arms around his neck. It felt wonderful to feel his strength against her. "Who became a wonderful man.''

"A man who's just learning to love, Dinah,'' he said, stroking her hair. "Business was something I grew up with. Music is something in my blood. But love, after all I'd seen happen to my family, was something new. Yet suddenly, there you were. A true princess. What could I do except love you? Will you come away with an up-and-coming commoner?''

"Not a commoner.'' She smiled. "The Emperor of All Nashville. A very prince of a fellow. And my own king of hearts.''

He bent his head and she kissed him happily and with all her being. She gloried in the hard and searching possession of his lips.

"You're so delicate, so rare," he whispered against her mouth. "Like a perfect little jewel. Flawless. And full of integrity and strength and fire.

"I love you as I never loved before. As maybe nobody has ever loved before."

He kissed her again, molding her against his body. "This must be right," she answered, pressing closer to him, "because you make me feel like I'm full of music. And it's all about you. I love you, Mitch."

Once more his lips took hers with hunger and mastery. "I'm going to marry you, you know," he warned her, his breathing uneven. "I suppose I knew that from the first, too, impossible as it seems. As much as I pretended otherwise. So just say yes, and please for once don't argue."

"I'm not arguing," she said. She rose on tiptoe so he could kiss her again.

Instead he nuzzled her neck. "You'll have to live in the reproduction of a mansion. But I guarantee the love will be real. And the bed will be square, not heart shaped."

"I don't care what shape the bed is," she said boldly, "as long as you're in it."

"Wench," he growled agreeably, nibbling her ear and making her shiver. His lips traveled to her breast, lingered there an intoxicating moment, then wandered back to her bare throat. "How do I get all these ruffles off you?" he asked, breathing raggedly. "More important—when? How I love you, Dinah! Come away with me—now. This minute. I didn't bring a ring. Will this do for now?"

Into her hand he slipped the box containing the diamond mousetrap. "Come away," he repeated, kissing her ear. "Now."

"Yes," she said. "Take me home."

"Don't even bring anything with you," he whispered. "Just the clothes on your back. Let me abduct you."

"I have to bring just one thing," she replied, kissing him back. "Roscoe's hat."

He looked at her in wry surprise. "Am I going to be haunted all my life by that incredible hat?" he asked, teasing her.

But she was not to be swayed. "It's Roscoe's lucky hat," she said, a catch in her voice. "And it's brought all of us too much luck and too much love to leave behind. I have to take it."

He kissed her, then arched his brow philosophically. "Just what every wife should come equipped with," he observed. "A diamond mousetrap and a cowboy hat."

"Exactly," she smiled up at him. "And now—take me home?"

"Yes, love," he said and kissed her again. "Home."

If **YOU** enjoyed this book,
your daughter may enjoy

Romances from

CROSSWINDS

Keepsake is a series of tender, funny, down-to-earth romances for younger teens.

The simple boy-meets-girl romances have lively and believable characters, lots of action and romantic situations with which teens can identify.

Available now wherever books are sold.

ATTRACTIVE, SPACE SAVING BOOK RACK

Display your most prized novels on this handsome and sturdy book rack. The hand-rubbed walnut finish will blend into your library decor with quiet elegance, providing a practical organizer for your favorite hard-or soft-covered books.

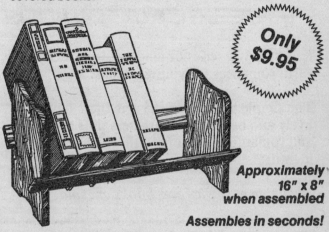

Only $9.95

Approximately 16" x 8" when assembled

Assembles in seconds!

To order, rush your name, address and zip code, along with a check or money order for $10.70* ($9.95 plus 75¢ postage and handling) payable to *Harlequin Reader Service*:

Harlequin Reader Service
Book Rack Offer
901 Fuhrmann Blvd.
P.O. Box 1396
Buffalo, NY 14269-1396

Offer not available in Canada.

BKR-1A

*New York and Iowa residents add appropriate sales tax.